MYSTERIES OF THE HEIGHTS

MYSTERIES OF THE HEIGHTS

CYRIL GEORGE JOSEPH

Quintus
An Imprint of ROMAN Books

Copyright © 2014 Cyril George Joseph

ISBN 978-93-80905-50-1

Typeset in Dante MT Std

First published in 2014

1 3 5 7 9 8 6 4 2

British Library Cataloguing in Publication Data.
A catalogue record for this book is available from the British Library.

Publisher: Suman Chakraborty

Quintus
An Imprint of ROMAN Books
26 York Street, London W1U 6PZ, United Kingdom
Suite 49, Park Plaza, South Block, Ground Floor, 71, Park Street, Kolkata 700016, WB, India
2nd Floor, 38/3, Andul Road, Howrah 711109, WB, India
www.quintus-books.co.uk | www.quintus-books.co.in

Printed and bound in India by
Repro India Ltd

This work is dedicated to Mother Teresa who turned the dust bowls of misery into the treasure troves of faith, hope and optimism.

1

On a turbulent evening, I returned to the heights where nature is always at her best. On account of the elevation that was well above sea level the chill in the air was appreciable. The streaks of lightning, crisscrossing the overcast sky, added an element of terror to the atmosphere.

As I negotiated the steep slope, the elegant silhouette of the church started emerging before my eyes. To stay away from the wrath of nature, I accelerated my steps. On reaching the top of the hillock, I paused for an instant and cast my eyes far and wide. The luxuriance of the landscape appeared amplified under the thick band of clouds. The peaks afar got partially hidden under the veil of moisture that heralded the onset of another spell of retreating monsoon, and the realisation sent shudders through my spine. At these heights, the north-east monsoon can present itself as an ugly customer; the lightning triggered by the clouds are capable of shattering into smithereens any hindrances on its way, and often the bosom of mother earth gets peeled off in the form of landslides. Many trees get uprooted in the forests, and the serene brook in the woods instantly transforms itself into a ruptured artery conveying the gush of flash floods.

The wind started to blow in gusts, and visibility dimmed considerably owing to the thick blanket of clouds. The nip in the air pierced the flesh, and started to gnaw at the bones. As the forerunner of rain, there was a roar in the horizon, and the apprehensions about the retreating monsoon propelled me to the vicarage.

Dazzle of lightning . . . followed by the violent cracking of thunder . . . curdled my blood. The deadly blow of the thunder must have pounded some corner of the valley. The vegetation near the vicarage swayed violently under a strong wind, and the whistle of the gusts suddenly turned into an unpleasant roar.

The thrust of the air brought me down onto the portico of the vicarage. Twigs and dry leaves slammed onto my face. The ugly face of nature put me out of my senses and filled the heart with an eerie feeling. Springing up in a flash, getting hold of the bell rope, I kept on pulling it like a totally disoriented person. The roar of the wind reached its zenith. With a pounding heart I cast a backward glance, and found the fury of nature charging at me with the destructiveness of a huge army.

The door opened, and I thrust myself in rather insolently; behind me the door slammed with a bang.

'What?' the gentleman who opened the door asked, with apparent annoyance, and I told him why I was there, in a few words.

'The vicar is upstairs and he is in prayers. He is expecting you. Please be seated 'He spoke politely, and it became evident that he knew that I would have come.

The vicarage rattled in the turbulence. It seemed the wind was all out to shatter the glass windows and twist the iron grills. Seated on a chair, I scanned every inch of the room. The furniture and other items were in ship shape, logs were burning in the fireplace, and at the exact centre of the room, on a table, a lantern burned faintly. The glass windows, frosted by the rain, obscured the view outside; the roar of the wind and the patter of the raindrops kept on intensifying.

'I am Esteppan . . . the vicar's assistant' The host introduced himself.

Through the correspondence of the vicar, I had already formed a clear picture of Esteppan, who was an orphan. His association with the vicar started many years back from a coastal hamlet in Kerala. Though the insecurity he felt as an orphan moulded Esteppan into an extreme introvert, his association with the vicar inculcated faint sparks of confidence in him.

8

Again the vicarage shuddered under the impact of a loud thunder, and the raindrops kept on battering the roof. It took a few moments for us to unshackle from the impact of thunder, and I felt the inadequacy of the walls and roof of vicarage to shelter us from the wrath of nature. Involuntarily my hand touched the cross on my bosom, and I prayed fervently to the Almighty for protection from the wild weather. Esteppan looked totally unsettled, shivering like a string that had been plucked.

I struggled against the chill in the air with knees and legs turning stiff.

'Could you please accompany me to the kitchen? I will make hot tea for you,' Esteppan said on observing my discomfort.

His reluctance to go into the kitchen alone was evident, so I decided to keep him company. Treading through the dark and long corridors, we reached the kitchen, and nature, through the raindrops, kept on percussing the tin roof over the room. The hot tea he gave me lifted my spirits and energy.

Suddenly the metal roof shook under a violent thud; Esteppan staggered back, and his shudder was obvious even in the faint glow of the lantern.

'Could be a branch fallen off the tree . . . let us go upstairs . . . the vicar must have finished his prayers' Uttering these words in a shaking voice, Esteppan leapt out of the kitchen. Leaving the cup on the table, I followed him.

We started climbing the steep wooden stairs. Esteppan held the lantern in his hand and helped me ascend throwing the flame onto the stairs. The willingness of the vicar to negotiate steep stairs at this advanced age left a positive impression in my mind.

In the gleam of the lantern, we struggled to ascend the stairs, and to keep my balance I fastened my fingers onto the wooden railing. Finally, we reached upstairs and proceeded to the prayer room.

In the candle light the little stature of the vicar, kneeling before the crucifix, emerged. In a corner of the room stood a person who was as alert as a guard, and he responded to the blows of nature on the vicarage by casting uneasy glances to the roof, intermittently.

The vicar was able to fasten his mind on the Almighty despite the raging turbulence, and with remarkable placidity he had engrossed himself in deep meditation. His spiritual communication with the Almighty remained unaffected despite the fury of the weather. His faith was firm as solid rock, and I enjoyed the sight immensely which increased my confidence tenfold.

Awakening from his meditation, the vicar made a futile attempt to stretch himself up. The person who was standing at the corner stepped forward and supported him. With a leaping heart I grabbed his hand. His face turned radiant at my sight, and with trembling fingers he touched my face. The pleasant waves of vibration which triggered from his hands radiated throughout my body, filling my heart to the brim. The eyes of the elderly vicar shone like celestial bodies; the exultant happiness drove him to the verge of tears, and on account of the sudden flood of emotion we gazed at each other in silence for a few moments.

Time had already stamped its impressions on the vicar, the wrinkles on the face, the encroachment of baldness, stooping head and sagging shoulders stood out, even in the faint light.

'How are you child?' He asked in a shivering, feeble voice.

'I am fine by the grace of God.'

The vicar introduced his subordinate 'Devassy', who was also a member of the trio headed by the vicar.

'This devilish nature is going to destroy everything' Devassy gave vent to his concern.

'Devassy . . . this is the profound sorrow of nature . . . let her have her outburst,' the vicar replied.

These words touched my heart and I felt the presence of hidden dimensions in the response of the vicar.

'What kind of rain is this?'

Esteppan also expressed his concern. The vicar smiled at me; the beauty, innocence and the truth in it captivated me immensely.

'Reunion with the loved ones can result in the outpouring of emotions . . . let her cry . . . let her cry again and again . . . and let her find consolation in this,' with quivering voice, the vicar replied.

I felt an apparent connection between my visit and the transformation in nature's mood, and as a result, seeds of fear and curiosity started germinating in my heart.

With the aid of a lantern we brought the vicar back to the ground floor overcoming the challenging steep descent of the stairs.

'He is very insistent on climbing the stairs every day despite enough room for prayer on the ground floor,' Esteppan voiced his annoyance and concern. The vicar responded with a pleasant smile. He started walking without support after reaching the ground floor, and it appeared he had recouped his strength by dint of prayer. He tossed some fragments of log into the fireplace. After an initial hesitation, the flames started to burn with vigour.

The rain kept on pouring incessantly, and the glare of the streaks running through the sky was reflected on the glass windows. There was a respite in the roar of thunder.

At the vicar's instruction, Esteppan guided me to the bedroom. Each and every inch of the vicarage appeared well-organized like the well-disciplined life of the vicar. The furniture had been fashioned out of majestic wood, the elegance of which was striking even in the insufficient light.

'This room commands an excellent view of the place,' commented Esteppan.

'Yes Esteppan . . . I had been a frequent visitor to this house in the past. I still have vivid recollections of the beautiful view this room commands'

'It's dinner time . . . let me go to the kitchen'

Esteppan hastened away from the room, and it was clear that the reason that prompted him to leave the room was the wish to stay close to the vicar and not the commitment to his calling.

I was alone in the bedroom. After changing into nightclothes, I clad myself in the comfort of the thick blanket. Like a well-orchestrated ballet, the shadows tottered with the vacillation of the flame. Against the wildness of incessant rain, I enjoyed the subtle, rhythmic movements of the shadows on the wall.

2

Right before my eyes, emerged a divinely beautiful landscape encircled by towering mountains. Aeons back, when the Almighty embarked on the process of creation, this landscape was moulded with extreme care and attention to the details. It is in the divinely inspired heights that nature reaches its completeness. The luxuriant tea gardens extending many square kilometres, the dense forests in the valley, the gurgling brooks and roaring waterfall are, all together, a feast for the eyes.

During the south-west monsoon the heights get enveloped in a thick blanket of clouds, the peaks are festooned with the silver of running water and the roar of the waterfall becomes audible even for many miles around. During winter the heights hide themselves in the thick veil of mist, and in summer the landscape is ablaze with colourful flowers. The rarefied air of this region is as sweet as honey, and when the viscous air flows into the lungs, the very cells in the body tend to throb on account of overflowing energy.

This is where I spent my boyhood after the relocation of my parents to the heights from the sultry tropical midlands of Kerala in connection with official duties. The official residence of my father located on top of a hillock commanded a panoramic view of the heights. At the end of summer huge chunks of clouds from the Arabian Sea start drifting towards the heights giving the impression of being only 'at an arm's length'. Finally, the cluster of monsoon clouds smashes onto the peaks unleashing heavy downpours.

Esteppan, who came with the invitation for supper, brought my thoughts back to the present. Rains accompanied by powerful winds kept on lashing without cease, and the frost on the glass windows thickened. With reluctance I bade adieu to the warmth of the blanket. I had been in the vicarage for the last two hours. The very thought of the destructiveness of the rain which lashed the heights throughout this time send shivers down my spine. Treading through the carpeted corridors, we reached the living room.

The vicar, fully clad in warm clothes, was seated beside the fireplace. Like a dangling shadow, Devassy stood behind him.

'Let us pray,' said the vicar.

I opened the Scriptures, and like divine intervention the gospel of Matthew blossomed before me. It had been my habit to open the Bible at random and I considered the lessons accessed in this manner as the culmination of a divine plan. This habit had been of great help to sight turbulence and take corrective actions, well in advance.

Based on the lesson, the vicar delivered a short sermon. Nature is the boon of the Almighty. Often the Almighty speaks through this medium. His intense rage lapped up the cities of Sodom and Gomorrah in the form of tongues of fire. He made the night which witnessed the birth of his beloved son extremely beautiful, and placed the brightest star in the sky to proclaim the good news to all the nations. When the son accepted death on the cross, even the earth trembled under the fury of the Supreme Being. After the short sermon, the vicar opened his heart and the waves of prayer appeared to be lashing on the gates of heaven.

After Prayer, Esteppan served the dinner consisting of hot rice gruel, baked beans and pappadam. The wind kept on howling like a pack of wolves, and the raindrops smashed onto the glass windows, without pause.

'My Goodness,' cried Estappan who was scared at such vagaries of nature.

'Devasy . . . is it fine at our dairy farm?' asked the vicar.

Devassy nodded affirmation.

'Child . . . do you remember our dairy farm?' asked the vicar.

The salutation 'Child', suffused with the overflowing affection of the vicar, amused me immensely. From his point of view, I am still a child, despite my pronounced manhood.

'Yes,' I responded.

'By the grace of God it is going well. . . . All the activities of the dairy farm are overseen by this Devassy'

The vicar touched the shoulder of Devassy with boundless affection. In response, he bowed his head in humility.

After dinner, we all moved to the living room and sat beside the fireplace.

For an instant, we were hypnotized by a powerful streak of lightning, and at the same time came the violent clap of thunder. We all turned stiff; the vicarage seemed to shiver under the impact, and Devassy and Esteppan each coiled like a leech in fear. Even the vicar, who was far superior to us in faith and courage, became speechless for an instant.

The chill kept on intensifying with the rains, and I clad every inch of my body in warm clothes.

'Do you know why tonight is important?' asked the vicar.

'No.'

'Tonight is the fifteenth death anniversary of Tresa.'

Devassy and Esteppan cast fearful glances at each other, the expressions on their faces not quite the same. They were under the severe grip of fear.

'Fifteen years back . . . an evening like this . . . it was as turbulent as tonight'

I clearly felt an uncomfortable heaviness in my heart, and sat speechless with intensifying sorrow. Tresa . . . the divine incarnate still lives in my heart.

She was as luminous as solar flares; her long golden hair used to cascade in the breeze, her presence was as aromatic as a divine flower, her beautiful eyes always carried the azure of the sky and her words were always soothing. She was the embodiment of nobility. Chiselled features, pleasing manners, striking gestures and dignified carriage. . . . She was an unique sculpture of the Almighty in all respects.

'In spite of the hostile weather, we embarked on a search. We searched the entire landscape with a fine-toothed comb.' The vicar came under the grip of powerful emotions; his lips distorted with grief, face convulsed, eyes turned tearful, and rate of breathing accelerated. 'Finally we were able to retrieve her body from the grasslands . . . brutally savaged by a wild beast.'

The vicar broke down. Somehow restraining my surfacing emotions I embraced and pressed him to my bosom. The well-respected, dignified vicar took to my bosom as a mere toddler. Even so, he regained his composure in a flash, and I sat back on the chair. But Devassy and Esteppan still remained shaken.

'She was like a beautiful rose squashed by a wild elephant.' In a shaking voice, the vicar put a stop to the narration. I sat speechless, the words remained entangled in the throat, and the heaviness in the heart kept on intensifying.

Suddenly the vicarage rattled under a loud explosion. Esteppan and Devassy leapt forward and grabbed the hands of the vicar, and we even feared that the vicarage was about to collapse. The atmosphere turned thick with the desperate wail of the animals and the thud of uprooted trees. The anguished wail of the wild prolonged for a few minutes and then faded away gradually. Outside the vicarage, only the howling of the rain and the wind prevailed.

'Landslides . . . you hear how the animals screamed? It seems many trees have been uprooted,' said Esteppan.

The explosion which engulfed and shook the heights to the core was caused by landslides brought on by heavy rains. Though the epicentre of the disaster was in the innermost part of the forest, the intensity was strong enough to travel many miles to rattle the vicarage to the foundation. Devassy and Esteppan sat with sagging shoulders and shivering hands. Even the flame of the lantern kept vacillating.

'Where is her tomb?'

After regaining composure I took the initiative to break the silence which was getting uneasy. Esteppan and Devassy both responded to the question with a violent start. I was astonished by the intensity of fear in their eyes, and it was quite clear that they wanted to avoid this discussion at any cost.

The vicar responded slowly, staring at me with languid eyes and said, 'In the cemetery of the church'

Again an uneasy silence flooded the room, the violence of nature went on uninterrupted, and I was astonished by the vagaries in the emotions of Esteppan and Devassy. They were fearful of something more intense than the turbulence raging outside. With stooping shoulders and closed eyes sat the vicar. After a while he raised his head and stared at me, then uttered in a quivering voice, 'This place is witnessing a few miracles after her death.'

An uneasy chill passed through my spine. With heightened curiosity, I bent forward, keeping my ears on high alert, and focused my attention completely on the vicar.

'Miracles?' I could not restrain the cry of amazement.

The winds blew strongly, the deadly series of pulverising streaks of lightning and ear-shattering thunderclaps went on for a few minutes. Every crack of thunder seemed determined to shatter the vicarage to smithereens; every streak of lightning looked set to pulverize it. We tried in vain to cocoon ourselves from the wrath of nature by coiling ourselves like leeches. Like fear-stricken kittens, we sat expecting the worst, and glancing now and again to the roof. Only the vicar remained unfazed. He was in possession of a faith grounded on a firm bedrock. He continued after a short pause.

'Her tomb is covered by a creeper which is always in full bloom. It is always adorned with beautiful flowers . . . very beautiful flowers'

'Why is that so special?'

'Because it is in full bloom around the clock, throughout the year . . . flowers that emit divine fragrance.'

'What kind of creeper is that?' My curiosity was sky high.

'That is totally unknown, to everyone . . . there are no parallels on the face of the earth . . . it is totally unseen and unheard of anywhere else in the world'

An unknown fear started to take possession of me, and the narration of the vicar turned out to be hair-raising.

'Is it a variant of Neelakurunji?' I asked in a quivering voice.

The vicar nodded his head negatively and once again the creepy silence gained prominence. Despite thick frost on the window, the glare of the lightning streaks appeared clearly, as a dance of lights.

'Last week a team of botanists paid a visit on behalf of the government. Even they are at a loss. Something like this has never, ever been recorded.'

'They have taken the sample of stems and leaves, it covers the tomb completely—it is in fact a flower bed'

My thoughts churned like a whirlpool. On one side is the violence of nature . . . on the other side is the narratives of unearthly events. The words uttered by the vicar after that lashed in my ears like thunder.

'Many sightings of the girl had been reported after her death—at night . . . near the cemetery . . . in the grasslands . . . at the edge of the forests.'

I sat spellbound, and started to sweat profusely despite the sharp nip in the air.

The horizons shivered under the impact of a loud thunder and the effect resonated through the windows of the vicarage. Esteppan sprang forward like a rabid dog, giving vent to some jarring utterances and gesticulating clumsily.

His face was taut under immense pressure. It was quite clear that he wanted to put a stop to the conversation. His eyeballs popped, tongue lolled, and breathing accelerated. Like a madman, Esteppan rambled about in the room for a few minutes. Finally, he ran forward, grabbed the vicar by the shoulders and shook him violently. He tried to say something in desperation, but the words came out only as moans and groans.

Fearing for the welfare of the vicar I pounced on Esteppan, and Devassy lent a hand and kept a tight hold on him. With the energy of a wild horse, he tried to break free. After immense physical exertions, we were able to bring him under control.

The vicar remained calm. Even in that awkward situation his countenance remained radiant.

'He is scared . . . there is nothing more to it than that . . . please release him,' said the vicar. We released him with some reluctance.

'Esteppan . . . where is your faith . . . what are you afraid of . . . are you ignorant of the fact that we are all under the protection of the Almighy?' asked the vicar.

Gradually, he eased off, then sat down, and placed his head on the vicar's lap. The vicar ran his fingers through his hair, and the touch of the saintly completed the cure.

The destructive spell of nature went on uninterrupted and the raindrops smashed onto the roof. The flame of the lantern swayed violently, raising the fear of its being extinguished.

'It is late . . . dear child, go to bed,' said the vicar. 'Let Esteppan sleep in my room . . . he is really worried'

The vicar proceeded to his room with unsteady steps, chanting the verses of Psalm 91. Like an obedient lamb, Esteppan followed him. The celestial verses recorded by the Psalmist thousands of years ago came drifting through the air. 'Live under the protection of God Most High and stay in the shadow of God all powerful. . . . Then you will say to the Lord You are my fortress, my place of safety, you are my God and I trust you' These beautiful verses fortified my self-confidence, and the glow of the psalms pushed the darkness of fear aside.

'The Lord will keep you safe from secret traps and deadly diseases. . . . He will spread his wings over you and keep you secure. . . . His faithfulness is like a shield or a city wall.'

His voice gradually started to thin out; the flawless protection of God overflowed the verses, and imbibing the verses and planting them in the bottom of my heart, I headed for the bedroom. The influence of the verses bolstered my confidence and effaced apprehensions.

The flame of the lantern glowed faintly in the bedroom and the windows remained fully frosted from the moisture. I plunged into the warmth of the blanket, and Devassy stretched himself in the corner with blankets and pillows. Listening to the melody of the raindrops, I reclined in the comfort of the bed and stared into the darkness. The hissing of the treetops in the gale was clearly audible. Seeds of fear started sprouting in my mind; fear crept into the heart like a venomous, deadly snake. With great effort, I brought the essence of Psalm 91 back to my heart. Slowly the turbulence subsided. Again I focused back on the melody and rhythm of nature. The howling of the wind synchronized perfectly with the battering of raindrops. Slowly I immersed myself into the harmony of nature.

In the distance the peaks peeled off the veil of mist, the radiance of the sun pierced through the canopy of treetops, dewdrops sparkled like diamonds and treetops rippled in the breeze. I was flying to an unknown destination. . . . When I glided just over the grasslands, the blades of grass stood upright and kissed my feet. With a velocity accelerating every second, I reached the edges of the dense forests. Through the thick canopy of branches and leaves I flew, twisting and turning. Gradually I gained dizzying heights. It was like an invisible hand lifting me to the elevation which commanded an extensive aerial view of hills, forests and tea gardens. Slowly, I drifted closer to the highest peak and traversed its summit. An unknown force elevated me again and I found myself engulfed by the clouds shivering in freezing vapour.

I started losing height and emerged from the cloud cover. Aided by the unknown hand, I plunged in a free fall onto the vast expanse of grasslands. My eyes spotted two figures darting through the steep valleys and entering the grasslands. It was a girl holding the hand of a boy and guiding him through the luxuriance of nature. Her golden hair cascaded in the wind, and like an angel she guided the child to an unknown world. The shepherds with their flocks at the valley appeared in my sight. The human forms dashed through the flocks and scattered them in all directions. The bleating of the sheep and calls of the shepherds were vivid and clear. They were heading for another world . . . a beautiful world even beyond our wildest imaginations . . . finally they grew smaller to mere blotches afar in the grasslands.

Gradually my vision started losing its sharpness. The grasslands, valleys and flocks blurred and smudged. The bleak canopy of the mist appeared faintly through the glass window studded with raindrops. In the faint morning light, Esteppan stood near me holding a cup of tea which threw curls of smoke up in the air.

3

The cold dull landscape blanketed in fog greeted me that morning. On account of the deep-rooted habit of taking a morning stroll every day, I set off early in the morning despite the entreaties of the vicar and Devassy. I clad myself in warm clothes to battle the challenges of the nearly freezing weather. Like a damsel covering her face in a veil, the landscape remained hidden in the translucency of mist. The subtle turns and twists of the fog in the gentle breeze captivated my mind. Visibility remained poor because of the fog in which the church complex and tall trees appeared as mere outlines.

I proceeded towards the church, and in the semi transparency of the mist the sun shone like a full moon. Prompted by piercing chill and poor visibility, I almost made up my mind to return to the vicarage, abandoning the stroll. Suddenly the mist began to thin out in a strong breeze that carried an unearthly, divine fragrance which I enjoyed immensely. The breeze gained momentum considerably, the fog started to move in circles, the rays of the sun got brighter, and the azure of the sky emerged gradually.

I stood facing the facade of the church. Since its inception, the parish have been a great blessing to the heights irrespective of caste, creed and religion. I sincerely prayed for the continuation of the blessing. Slowly the horizon emerged, treetops came into clear sight and the gentle warmth of sunbeams replaced the needling chill.

That moment, I became the sole witness of a strange phenomenon. Peeled off from the four corners of the sky, aided by a strange centripetal force, the mist started to swirl around and enveloped the church. Then slowly the wind pushed the blanket of fog and foundations appeared . . . stonewalls, pillars, slanting roof, and belfry emerged in strict sequence. Finally, the wind tore away the envelope of the mist from the structure and right in front of my eyes, the elegant edifice of the church unveiled fully.

The windows and doors were made of excellent wood, and the cherubic images engraved on the doors looked flawless. I cast my eyes wide and enjoyed the sight of the tea gardens rolled out like a green carpet up to the towering peaks.

'Nothing has changed,' I said to myself.

I was very impressed with the way mother earth had preserved her beauty, and a few seconds later I found myself treading the narrow tracks intersecting the tea gardens. It was many years since I traversed the veins of the tea gardens through which the beauty of nature courses abundantly. At frequent intervals I met labourers coming from the opposite direction and stepped aside for them, and they walked past me, casting questioning glances.

The turbulence of the previous night had left its deadly footprint on the landscape, and I kept on moving forward with utmost care since the surface remained extremely slippery in the wake of rains. Festoons of running streams which adorned the peaks glistened in the bright sunshine—these are the scenes which always appear at the heights after heavy downpour.

I advanced through the tracks which led to an elevated surface girdled by rocks, and my position was nearly two kilometres east of the church.

The elevated surface commanded an excellent view of the landscape. On the west stood the elegant structure of the church. On the east there was the green carpet of grasslands and thick bamboo groves rolled out by nature. Afar, the towering peaks stood cloud-capped, and sunlight percolated onto the forest floor through the thick canopy of leaves and branches.

Thin patterns of smoke kept curling up from the gully between the rocks. The cave there had been my favourite resting place in my childhood. In summer, due to the passage of furious winds, the cave turns itself into a flute, breathing out ear-pleasing melodies. I always nursed a desire to return to the cave and listen to the purest melodies of nature. But the cave had an encroacher. A kind of resentment started bubbling in my heart since I always considered the grotto as my own place, and I felt quite certain that the encroacher would have been either a poet or a naturalist.

I plunged myself into the luxuriance of the vegetation and waded through the thick undergrowth, completely ignoring the threat of poisonous reptiles. The soft touch of nature and the aroma of tender blades of vegetation led me to celestial bliss. Involuntarily my arms moved and I swam through the dense flora. In constant rhythm, unaided, my feet moved.

Right in front of me emerged the overflowing brook. The branches touching the surface of the flowing water still swayed from the shock of last night's torrential rain. On the other side of the brook stood the thick fortification of a dense forest.

I tried to penetrate my vision through that dense wall of vegetation. Teak, mahogany and rosewood, the noble subjects of the plant kingdom, stood sky high, proudly, and the green wall of nature appeared impregnable. I stood spellbound, on the banks of the brook, completely absorbed in the purest music of nature. On one side were the towering trees, on the other side the thick sheet of grass and bamboo trees. Suddenly the gentle breeze stopped and the entire landscape froze at the musical notes of the torrent.

The golden hair flying in the breeze . . . beautiful loose garments swaying in the air. A celestial apparition plunged into the depths of luxuriance of nature. The presence of that goddess sanctified the landscape; the branches stretched themselves desperately to scrape against the angel, and the greenery throbbed with the desire to press her to the bosom affectionately. Gradually the apparition melted completely into the luxuriance of the landscape.

The violent trumpeting of a wild elephant from the interior of the forest knocked me up from the world of reveries and prompted me to turn back at once. I found Esteppan near the facade of the church, waiting with impatience. He was there to take me to the Tresa's tomb, at the vicar's instruction.

We arrived at the huge entrance of the cemetery which was nearly two-hundred metres away from the church complex. Esteppan inserted the old iron key into the lock and flicked his wrist anticlockwise. The lock opened with a click. We pushed the huge iron gates open and stepped into the two-centuries old extensive cemetery that entombs the remains of the British who came to the heights during the time of colonial rule.

Right in front of us lay the extensive plateau dotted with thousands of tombs and headstones. Through the knee-deep grass, Esteppan led me forward, and with careful steps we advanced into the inmost parts of the cemetery.

The cloud flakes drifting in the sky darkened the tombstones and the grass. It was possible to get a clear view of the tallest peak in the heights from the cemetery. The cloud-capped peak had always been noted for its elegance. When we reached the rear parts of the cemetery, a patch that reminded me of red silk appeared in a corner, and struck our vision like a lightning.

Suddenly my olfactory sense was stimulated by a strange fragrance. It kept on intensifying at every step, and I felt the gentle touch of the divine which relieved my nerves from stress and agony.

'There it is,' Esteppan pointed his finger towards the red patch, and with a racing heart, I stepped forward. The tomb of Tresa was covered with the creeper, and the luxuriance of the flora even obscured the headstone. It was laden with beautiful flowers and appeared like diamond studs on green velvet. I was engrossed in this beautiful sight and the agony that lingered in my mind on account Tresa's untimely demise was momentarily effaced.

I sat on a stone slab beside the tomb; the expression in the eyes of Esteppan bespoke fear, and it seemed his mindset was a far cry from the pleasant experience I was having.

'Let us go,' Esteppan hastened to go back.

'Esteppan . . . please proceed . . . let me spend some time here.'

Esteppan returned at once; obviously he was under the grip of fear.

I was alone in the cemetery and watched the flowerbed closely. The flowers were trumpet-shaped, bright red in colour and the size of the palm. The profusion of flowers hid the leaves and stems and formed a flower bed over the tomb.

The blades of grass murmured and fluttered in the breeze, and to shield myself from the sharpening nip I snuggled myself in the warmth of the shawl. The fragrance, which intensified every moment, soothed my strained nerves. With an arching bosom, I inhaled the fragrance to the fullest possible extent.

The sunbeams strengthened, intensifying the blue tint of the towering peaks. Fully engrossed in the fragrance, in the radiance of the flower bed, I sat totally oblivious of the surroundings.

4

I remember vividly, as if it all happened yesterday. It started with the relocation of my parents to the heights from the midlands of Kerala when I was a seven-year-old. One afternoon, we paid a visit to the residence of one of our family friends who was a towering figure in the heights. His large house on top of a hillock had extensive grounds enclosed by high granite walls; many flower-laden creepers snaked up to the roof through the exterior walls of the house, and the pot plants which dotted the facade were adorned with floral crowns. In short, the house and its precincts were ablaze with the superabundance of flowers. The interiors were also as elegant as the exterior. Tiled floors, glass windows, furniture fashioned out of elegant woods, well-carpeted rooms, the majestic flight of wooden stairs lined with railings leading to the first floor. . . .

The stairs began to creak gently under soft footsteps.

'Here's our daughter,' said our family friend pointing his arm towards the wooden stairs. I cast my glance in that direction, and that is where my clearest memories had their origin.

She appeared like a flame descending the stairs, and in its intense radiance, I struggled to keep my eyelids peeled. There appeared a girl of celestial beauty, clad in a beautiful flowing dress. Her golden hair cascaded down to her knees, and her eyes carried an unearthly glow. She was descending the stairs with a smile which was as beautiful as moonlight. Our family friend introduced his daughter to us with a few words.

He requested her to shake my hand, and she drifted towards me like a gentle breeze. Involuntarily, unknowingly, I sprang forward from the seat. Her palm, which unfolded before me, was as elegant as marble, and I felt as if a garland of flowers encircling my palm, when mine completely enfolded in hers.

'Please show him around,' said her mother. I discreetly compared our heights and found her about a foot taller than me.

We ascended the stairs, making the wooden steps squeak; Tresa floated like a flame, and guided me through the labyrinthine corridors of the elegant house. Like a moth hallucinated by the glow of the lamp, I followed her with swaying, unsteady steps. She showed and explained the intricate details of the pictures hanging on the wall. Some of the pictures had the backdrop of beautiful English landscape. After a few days, I came to know that the branches of her family tree went as far across as England, Ireland, and Scotland. We descended the stairs and through the rear door stepped out.

On account of the elevation, the precincts of her house commanded a panoramic view of the landscape. Hills carpeted in green, flakes of cloud scraping against the towering peaks, and the curls of mist rising from the abyss in the valley. Since I was unaccustomed to the high-range weather, I was well clad in warm clothes.

I enjoyed the scenery in astonishment. Like an angel, she guided me to the orchard and presented innumerable flowers, fruit trees and plants before me. Then we circled the elegant house, and she whispered in my ears the intricate details of the creepers which appeared like flower garlands growing up to the sky. Finally, we drifted towards the abundance of pine trees; in the uneven terrain I struggled to maintain the balance and she grabbed my hand sensing to lend support. I felt the softness of a lotus apparently swallowing my arm, and the bliss I experienced in her presence was beyond words.

The pine trees swayed in the wind, the thin veil of mist that enveloped us thickened and thinned at the whim of nature. I felt a tickling sensation when her golden hair drifting in the air gently scraped against my face, and a celestial aroma filled the surroundings. For the first time in my life, I felt celestial bliss and divine peace. We circled the building once again and reached the back of the house. Hillocks and lofty peaks remained fully obscured under the thick blanket of fog. Throughout the stroll on foot, my hand remained firmly enclosed in the lotus which had shrunk for me. Unaware of the passage of time, we stood, fully engrossed in the fickleness of nature and the flame beside me shone intensely in spite of poor light.

Someone knocked me up from the reveries and with a start, I returned to the present. Esteppan was standing beside me, and it was nearly two hours since I placed myself near the flower bed.

5

The news about the embarkation of the vicar on an intense fasting prayer took me by surprise. It became apparent that a fasting prayer of such severity would have been prompted by incidents of utmost seriousness. After a hasty lunch, I proceeded to the prayer room on the first floor. The vicar was on his knees and was meditating with closed eyes, perfectly still. He had always unlocked puzzles and problems by driving himself to extremes through severe fasting prayers.

The excruciating pain he endured at heart was evident on his face. Devassy, who was keeping guard in the prayer room, remained on high alert and his services to the vicar seemed praiseworthy. Finally, I withdrew myself from the prayer room.

The inexplicable, unearthly creeper carpeting the tomb, the dreams unfolding even in light slumber and finally the incidents which pushed the vicar into an intense fasting prayer—mysteries . . . riddles . . . the paranormal. . . . My mind was in absolute turbulence. Finally, a place to clarify all these enigmas came to mind, and I yearned to reach there at the earliest on account of growing worries. I set off after giving a clear description of my destination to Esteppan.

The sun was slanting west, and the nip in the air was intensifying. I put on an extra shield against the chill by covering the chest with a shawl. The breeze carried the aroma of tea powder, and the evening sun painted the landscape gold. The play of the elements of nature brought the verses of psalm 104 drifting into my heart, and I thanked the Almighty who crafted nature with such abundant beauty. I travelled through one of the many narrow capillaries intersecting the carpet of tea gardens.

Not far away, on top of a hillock, appeared the faith home, where the activities of my bosom friend Yohannan were centred. He belonged to a middle-class family of farmers who had migrated from the midlands of Kerala.

It was nearly twelve years since we met last, but throughout this period, regular correspondence with each other had strengthened the relationship. He was a missionary in the faith home, gifted with an excellent sense of humour. I firmly believed Yohannan was capable of allaying my apprehensions.

The light breeze laced with the aroma of tea powder eased the strain on my heart. I had been ignorant of the presence of the divine in nature and cared nothing for the subtle emotions. Like a well-automated system, the seasons had been appearing and disappearing, and I had never been able to comprehend the intricate messages communicated through the changefulness of nature. From the day before, nature appeared to convey cryptic messages in symbols. The expressions of nature in the form of battering rain and howling winds appeared meaningful; the flower bed carpeted the tomb; the gentle breeze embraced the landscape and swaying tree tops looked as though they were throbbing to reveal some mystery.

I ascended the gentle slope and proceeded to the top of the hillock through an avenue edged with fruit trees which stood as a testimony to the incessant labour of the missionaries. I asked the gardener, and he directed me to the hall since that was the place where Yohannan conducts the Bible Quiz.

The loud laughter of children greeted me at the hall, and I peeped through the window with curiosity, to find nearly one-hundred children seated on the floor. In one glance I recognized Yohannan, who was standing on the dais, with the same physique he had twelve years back—lean, dark and short.

Dressed in the lily-white traditional outfit of Mundu and Jubba, Yohannan stood out in the hall and his shawl, lay bundled on the desk. It was evident that the Bible Quiz was not going well, and the situation appeared totally uncontrollable with Yohannan struggling to keep his composure. The recklessness of the children annoyed him.

'Children . . . please participate seriously,' Yohannan screamed at the top of his voice, and the noise of the children eased a bit.

'Last question . . . last question,' Yohannan tried to calm the children down, and they waited for the last question.

'For the first time . . . for the first time . . . for the first time . . . in the garden of Eden.' Yohannan roused the curiosity of the children, with proper modulation and well placed pauses.

'What did Adam say to Eve when he met her first in the garden of Eden?' Yohannan launched the question perfectly.

Complete silence reigned in the hall and all remained speechless. The success in cornering the children lifted Yohannan's spirit, and with the body language of a victor, he pointed to the different corners of the hall. After succeeding in gagging the children, and placing the question paper on the desk, he stood on the dais with arms crossed, looking like one of the portraits of maharajas. Finally, with some reluctance a small child raised his hand.

A spasm of new energy flowed into Yohannan; beaming with enthusiasm he launched into the other children.

'Look at him,look at him, look at this tiny child . . . do you know anything other than making noise?' Yohannan continued in a soft voice, after cornering the children with his verbal darts.

'Dear child . . . please say the answer.'

The answer dropped like a bomb shell. 'I Love You.'

The hall shook under the laughter. Even I could not suppress my mirth. Yohanan sweated profusely and absolute pandemonium prevailed in the hall.

The child who gave the funny answer darted out, and others followed. Yohanan sat on the dais; frustration and disappointment rushed back onto his face, and covering his face with his palm he sat still, disoriented, for a few moments. Suddenly he became alert and looked around to ensure there were no witnesses to the setback he suffered. At my sight, he gave a start, then with apparent embarrassment, and hesitation, approached me.

I tried to greet the loser with a beautiful smile. He came closer, stared at my face for a moment, and in the next instant, we embraced each other, and with a heavy Malayalam accent he said, 'My God'.

We left the hall and headed for the lodgings of Yohannan. In the short stroll, we exchanged news of the last twelve years. I knelt, took off the footwear at the entrance of the lodgings of the missionaries and was about to straighten myself.

'Devil . . . Get Lost,' came the scream from the lodging like a thunder. Under the impact of the scream, I almost lost my balance and clung on to my companion involuntarily. Yohannan latched on to the door, and saved both of us from a bad fall. The shout was like a slap on our face, and Yohannan stepped into the lodging angrily.

'Don't test the Lord,' came another gust of shout that made it evident that the violent screams were not directed at us. With a sigh of relief, I followed Yohannan.

'Pastor,' Yohannan shouted back.

'Yes,' came the response after a slight pause.

'Why did you scream?' asked Yohannan. A figure emerged from the interior slowly. Yohannan pulled a chair roughly and threw himself onto it. The figure which emerged was short and fat. His eyes sparkled like stars and the distorted mouth bespoke intense curiosity.

'Dear Son . . . why are you so angry?' He tried to defuse the tension with soothing words.

'Why did you scream?' Yohannan blurted out.

'I was preparing the sermon for tomorrow. The theme centres around the temptation in the wilderness . . . the devil trying to tempt Our Lord.'

I struggled to conceal my amusement, and Yohannan somehow managed to restrain his temper. The man, like a cunning crow, shook his head and threw cursory glances sideways at regular intervals. It was quite clear he was as cunning as a jackal.

'Dear Son . . . how was the Bible Quiz?' He fired the harpoon of sarcasm at Yohannan. My companion turned a deaf ear to the question and stared into another direction.

'Moses descending from Mt Sinai with stone tablets heard battle cry from the camp of Israel . . . likewise a few minutes back I heard a battle cry from the hall.'

Yohannan turned pale. His opponent continued . . . 'Moses shattered the tablets and silenced the camps. Likewise I too thought of coming down to the hall and shattering the cheeks of those brats.'

It became evident that the opponent was far superior to Yohannan in terms of sense of humour. The opponent went on, 'I went out, then came the charging army of our children. They reminded me of the charging chariots of the pharaoh heading for the Red Sea. It seems our children are more ferocious than the army of pharaoh . . . to save his people from charging chariots, God parted the Red Sea . . . to save myself from the trampling of these senseless idiots I parted the door panels and jumped inside . . . our children's flight was really incredible . . . dear Yohannan are you in good health?'

The harpoon of scathing criticism shattered the pride of Yohannan, and he remained quiet like a volcano about to erupt. His breathing grew fast. I pushed myself to extremes to control the bursting laughter. The opponent spoke well, no doubt. 'Dear Yohannan . . . don't worry, it happens . . . furthermore you are young . . . you conduct the next quiz . . . but I recommend strongly that you do it under my supervision,' said the opponent.

He made most of the opportunity. Yohannan remained fully transfixed, on account of the humiliation.

'I will demonstrate how to conduct the Bible Quiz.'

The opponent continued to annoy Yohannan, who sprang from the chair angrily. The chair swayed back. He dragged me along, rushed to his room and slammed the door, transmitting the vibrations onto the window frames. Yohannan regained his composure in a short span of time.

Then we indulged in a long and winding conversation that drifted through our childhood, youth, parents, siblings, past, present and future. The light was gradually fading outside, and from the adjacent hall came the prayers and hymns of the missionaries. From the interiors of the forests came the toot of an elephant that was loud enough to curdle our blood.

When the conversation paused for a while, I presented the enigma of Tresa, and Yohannan turned pale in an instant. He left the room in an insolent manner which astonished me greatly. I realized the surfacing of fear in myself. After a while, Yohannan came back with a lighted lantern, and the flame pushed darkness away. Like a wounded tiger preparing to pounce back, darkness confined itself to the corners of the room.

I could read the mix of fear and nervousness in his eyes. He refused to discuss this topic in the evening, and to defuse the awkward situation, he put forward the suggestion of a trip to the lake in the forest. His suggestion was music to my ears since I had always yearned for a journey to the lake which overflowed with the bounties of nature.

I decided to leave as it was growing late, and politely turned down Yohannan's offer to accompany me back to the vicarage. We embraced each other and bade adieu in the name of the Almighty; then I headed for the vicarage.

I stepped into the beautiful landscape painted with silver, and the intensity of moonlight encouraged me to travel back without a lantern. Above the towering peaks appeared the moon which appeared brighter and bigger than usual, and the cloud-free sky was studded with thousands of stars. I left the boundary of faith home and started treading through one of the narrow paths that intersected the tea gardens.

The gentle breeze tickled the tea bushes and swayed the silver oaks. The shawl which covered my chest ballooned up in the thrust of air which induced in me a feeling of drifting in the wind like a bird. The tea garden was coated with silver and the entire landscape appeared like an ideal setting for the romantic scenes fashioned by nature.

Finally, I reached the walls of the cemetery which bordered the tea gardens, and that night the walls stood like a fortress before me. I noticed a crevice formed by falling granites at the top of the wall. An irresistible temptation to peep into the cemetery through the crevice took possession of me. After a slight hesitation, I headed towards that part.

After some physical exertions, I reached the top of the wall and turned back, maintaining the balance by holding on to both sides of the crevice. Afar stood the peaks glistening in the moonlight, and the silver-coated carpet of tea shrubs remained extended to the borders of the vicinity. For a few moments, I was totally engrossed in the beauty of nature.

I looked into the cemetery; thousands of tombs and headstones appeared before me; the flower bed which carpeted the tomb of Tresa shone brightly in the moonlight, and just behind the cemetery appeared the elegant church complex and the tall belfry.

The grass blades murmured in the breeze which brought forth the fragrance of rare flowers covering the tomb, and it was enough to unwind all the worries. Nature coated the creations of the Almighty with silver and set forth a feast for the eyes. Under the influence of the beauty of nature, I remained totally oblivious of the surroundings.

All of a sudden, the moonlight dimmed, and in a flash, a blanket of darkness started enveloping the surroundings. Curious about the untimely demise of the moonshine, I turned back. Over the peaks, the mist, like a strange phenomenon, was encircling and eclipsing the moon gradually. As the forerunner of disaster, a strong wind started lashing about in which the grass blades in the cemetery began to hiss like venomous snakes. The mist kept on growing every second and finally eclipsed the moon completely. Nature stood like a lantern with flames lowered.

The mist, then, gliding through the slopes of the peaks, landed on the carpet of the tea gardens, rebounded like a rubber ball and grew sky-high like a column of smoke. From the interiors of the forests howled wild dogs and wolves that brought me under the grip of an unusual fear in which my heart throbbed like a drum. The ground rattled in a tremor that sounded like a huge juggernaut with millions of wheels rolling over the crust of the earth. The howling reached its zenith and echoed all over the heights. The phenomenon charged towards me like a giant wave, and I tried in vain to scream. The intensity of fear choked my voice. The phenomenon spilled over the tea gardens, after obscuring the peaks.

My body startled under fear, legs swayed, and made me unstable. To avoid a fall, I held firmly on to the edges of the gap. The pet dogs in the heights also started howling and the fearful noise that symbolizes death reached its pinnacle. The tremor reached its zenith, the land shivered under its impact pushing a few granite blocks down from the wall of the cemetery. The experience seemed like a huge, ugly steam engine belching out thick fumes and hurtling towards me, rattling the landscape.

Like an octopus with a thousand tentacles, the phenomenon charged at me, overwhelming my sight with horrifying bleakness. In a flash, the deadly, amorphous form of mist landed on me, and the molecules of vapour chanted the mantras of evil. I felt within an ace of death, closed my eyes in fear, and tried in vain to scream at the top of my voice. The wind intensified with the determination to blow me away and to counter it, I tightened my grip on the edges of the crevice.

It appeared that the strange phenomenon was about to crush me to the pulp, and I cried to the Lord from the bottom of my heart. The mist chained me tightly, inflicting an excruciating pain of thousands of needles piercing my skin. The heights shivered and shuddered under the howling of the wild, and I continued praying fervently to the Almighty.

The devilish music of wilderness started to fade, the intensity of the rattling eased off, and I opened my eyes fearfully. The phenomenon was thinning out, bringing forth the moonlight gradually; the rim of the moon reappeared over the peaks, again the landscape emerged as silver coated, and the howling of dogs died down. I turned back. Like a sharp dissecting knife the towering bell tower sliced the phenomenon into two parts and the fragmented portions started hurtling away in several directions.

At a strange noise I redirected my gaze downwards, and to my amazement found a group of people walking towards me. I descended from the wall, a little embarrassed, and answered their questions coated with scepticism. The fear and frustration in them were apparent but they appeared relieved on learning that I was the vicar's guest. They were the members of the parish council returning after a meeting, but had lost their bearings in the intensity of the phenomenon that had enveloped the heights.

'Strange forces are at work,' They all said in one voice and prompted me to return to the safety of the vicarage. Under their intense persuasion, I headed for the vicarage without further ado.

6

At the vicarage, Esteppan and Devassy received me anxiously. The vicar, who was weary on account of the fasting prayer, was asleep. In passing, Esteppan alluded to the visit of the members of the parish council for an emergency meeting.

'What calls for an emergency meeting at this hour?' I asked.

'The vicar will tell you,' said Devassy evasively.

After dinner, I informed Esteppan about my plans to visit the reservoir and he volunteered to make arrangements for the morning.

On reaching the bedroom, I became aware of my racing heart. The influence of the phenomenon which went past the heights had indeed been profound. I unfolded the scriptures in the gleam of the lantern. An unearthly energy, imparted by the scriptures, was transmitted through my fingers and overwhelmed every cell of my body. Under its influence, my heart leapt and it infused an unearthly peace in my mind which symbolized the protection of the divine. Like a blooming lotus, the pages turned, and trusting completely in God, without any prior planning, I concentrated on one chapter.

With the ease of putting out a flame, the sun burned out. The demise of the sun made the moon lifeless; myriad stars and celestial bodies got shattered and scattered. Their fragments swished through the atmosphere leaving fiery trails and slammed onto the earth. Suddenly the entire universe rattled under the toot of a trumpet, and the sign of the son of God appeared in the horizons. The entire human race was summoned before him from the four corners of the earth, and the son of God assumed the throne for the final judgement. No longer prevailed seasons, days, and time—instead, only the divine bliss of eternal life, or the excruciating flame of everlasting fire. The human race, divided into two halves, stood on the left and the right of the king. Then came the final verdict. . . .

The son of God said to those on the right, 'Come, you are blessed by my father, inherit the kingdom prepared for you from the creation of the world. For I was hungry, and you fed me, I was thirsty, and you gave me a drink, I was a stranger and you invited me into your home, I was naked and you gave me clothing, I was sick, and you cared for me, I was in prison and you visited me.'

'Then these righteous ones will reply, "Lord when did we ever see you hungry and feed you? Or thirsty and give you something to drink? Or a stranger and show you hospitality? Or naked and give you clothing? When did we ever see you sick or in prison and visit you?" And the king will say, "I tell you the truth, when you did it to one of the least of these my brothers and sisters, you were doing it to me."'

Suddenly my heart galloped with powerful emotions, like electrified coils; my hair stood on end. I had read and reread this passage many times, but never had I imbibed the meaning so intensely, never . . . ever . . . had my heart throbbed so vehemently. Many times had I encountered the poor, the naked and the desperate and turned a blind eye to them, turned a deaf ear to their pain-stricken cries. Never before had I realized that the naked, the poor and the desperate I brushed aside ruthlessly was the Almighty Himself. With a start, I realized that the son of God who became poor, naked and suffered persecution for me is still poor, naked and being persecuted. I now associated all the people I had ignored in the past with him. The Christ is still poor, naked and in pain, pleading before me for mercy.

My mind was unsettled, heart fluttered, and eyes turned tearful. I thanked the Almighty for the conveyance of the truth, and in prayer I promised that the poor, the naked and the persecuted would not be sidelined by me anymore. I decided to associate myself with their sufferings, wants and pain. I heaved a sigh of relief after the prayer, and got up from the floor with tear-stained cheeks and lightened heart.

I cast a glance through the window and found the landscape incredibly beautiful in the full moon. I enjoyed the serenity and divinity of the sight profoundly.

Esteppan completed the arrangements for my journey in the morning itself; the rucksacks, cane sticks, food packets, water and knife all figured in the lengthy list of provisions gathered by him, and stood testimony to his meticulousness. I braced myself for the journey after prayers and a quick breakfast. I grew uneasy at the news that the vicar had entered another spell of rigorous fasting prayer. Before departing for the reservoir I visited the Prayer Room on the upper floor and found the vicar on his knees, fully engrossed in prayer with tear-stained cheeks. I became curious to explore what was pushing the vicar to such extremes and bade adieu to Devassy, who was standing in a corner of the room guarding the vicar. Esteppan accompanied me for a while telling me how to reach the spot where Yohannan was supposed to be waiting.

I accelerated my steps and inhaled the dense, pure and honey like air of the heights which infused considerable energy into the body. The legs, arms and every cell throbbed with vigour and appeared well prepared for any mission, no matter how difficult it was. I strictly followed the directions given by Esteppan and kept on forging ahead through the narrow path passing through the forest. The cave which exhales music with the swirl of the wind was in the vicinity of the path, and as I proceeded I found curls of smoke rising from the cave filtering up through the tree tops. It was evident that the culinary activities of the encroacher were in full swing.

Suddenly, appeared in the middle of the path something akin to a human being, and the fact that it was a feminine image amazed me a lot, but I still proceeded without slowing my pace. At every step, the figure became sharper and bigger, and she was dressed in blouse and Kaili extending only up to her knees. It was apparent that she was waiting for someone and stood like a huge fortress in my way. Surprised at my sight, she gave a violent start. With determined, firm steps, I moved forward. Suddenly, she leapt and disappeared into the cave like a rabbit. There was a small child near the entrance of the cave which was covered with a sackcloth and the outline of the woman remained visible through the screen. I walked past the entrance of the cave casting involuntary backward glances now and again.

A few metres from the cave, the path snaked into the dense forest. Yohannan was waiting under a huge tree. With prayers on our lips, we smashed the green wall of vegetation and plunged into the depths of the forest. The tools provided by Esteppan turned out handy and we slashed the branches and jungle vines down and waded through the thick vegetation. The cane helped us to maintain the balance, and to negotiate the hostile uneven terrain. After the recent rains, the forest looked more luxuriant than ever with a thriving undergrowth, and many springs overflowed along the bed of the forest. In the face of threats posed by reptiles, we stepped carefully, and slowly made our way through the dense flora. The thick canopy of tall trees prevented the percolation of sunbeams considerably, and so, despite bright sunshine, there was only dim light in forest.

The mob of monkeys protested against our presence by making jarring screeches, and for nearly two hours we kept inching through slowly. Finally, the luxuriance of vegetation started thinning out, and sunbeams started filtering through the green canopy with relative ease. The moisture-laden breeze indicated the presence of water, and suddenly we found ourselves near a thick, tall screen of vines stood like a bastion determined to halt our progress. Yohannan parted them ruthlessly and made a hole through which we could squeeze, and the azure of the lake appeared through the hole. We pushed ourselves in through the narrow gap and right before us stretched the vast reservoir.

Nature had rolled out a beautiful feast before us in the form of the reservoir which appeared like a sapphire studded on green. On one side of the reservoir stood one of the thickest forests on earth, and on the other side stretched the beautiful tea gardens. The lion's share of precipitation slamming onto the peaks flows down to the reservoir, and that is where the wild animals come to quench their thirst. The moist breeze enveloped us with a soothing embrace and the pure dense air, pristine clear water, and the lush green surroundings effaced the weariness of the long journey. While we walked briskly along the banks the rippling water rushed forth and kissed our feet, and the coolness stepped up our vigour. The beauty of nature appeared intoxicating and under its influence we both darted ahead, and the lashing wind brushed our faces. Our brisk movements lasted for a few minutes and finally, we threw ourselves down on the carpet of grass. I realized my heart was pounding like a drum, and we were quite literally under the intoxication of nature.

Flakes of cloud drifted through the air, aided by strong gusts the ripples in the reservoir tried to encroach the land. Immersed in nature, in the serenity, and in heavenly peace, we sat totally oblivious of the surroundings.

7

On the banks of the lake, in the lap of overflowing natural beauty, Yohannan opened his heart and narrated the incident which had left a lasting impression on his life.

Yohannan's parents, whose roots were in Central Travancore, had relocated to the heights with the intention of starting a new life by farming on the ranges. They disposed of the property at their native place and purchased land in the heights where coffee, cardamom, clove and other spices thrived. The first years after the migration were smooth and prosperous, enabling them to harvest 'gold' from the soil. Then came a series of setbacks: the harvest failed on account of natural calamities three years in a row and these events disrupted the rhythm of their life. Deepening financial liabilities drove the father out of his senses; he refrained from family prayers and enslaved himself to alcohol. Once a symbol of joy and prosperity, the little household later became a hell of skirmishes and rude words. Yohannan was only eight years old during those days of turbulence.

One night Yohannan was knocked up from deep sleep by an excruciating pain and breathlessness which lasted for a few seconds. He never knew that he was about to witness the most shocking incident in his life. Like an agitated serpent, the towering figure of his father, who was under the influence of alcohol, hissed and charged at him. His mother tried her best to deter her husband from harming the child. She fought like a tigress for the safety of Yohannan.

Such were the doings of the head of the household who was totally deranged by the unexpected free fall into the abyss of debt. When all corrective measures failed, he wanted to kill himself after wiping off his family. His intention was to kill his son first, who was in deep sleep, by choking him with a pillow, and then his wife.

On account of his wife's resistance, finally he was forced to withdraw. After a while, he regained his composure and wept profusely in penitence. His sobbing wife laid her hand on his head and prayed fervently, and under the influence of prayer he gradually regained normalcy.

Next morning, the gnawing pain of hunger awakened Yohannan. His father had left the house before the break of dawn, and the sufferings of her son prompted the mother to leave the house to try and stave off the raging hunger. There were dark patches under her eyes and her cheeks bore the stains of tears. With windswept hair and tattered dress, she walked through the winding, steep paths of the heights with unsteady steps. Finally, she succeeded in securing a few fragments of yam through incessant pleading, which provided relief to Yohannan temporarily.

There was nothing edible in the house for herself, not even a pinch of jaggery, not even a grain of rice, and not even a molecule of sugar. Yohannan experienced the stinging darts of poverty, and throughout the day prayed his mother tearfully. The father returned in the evening, again fully intoxicated, with face bearing the dark tint of distress and eyes devoid of hope. With overwhelming pain in heart, he watched his tired son who was asleep, and wife who was praying fervently. It was getting dark over the heights, and indoors, a lean, unstable flame, weak enough to burn out anytime, struggled to push the annoying darkness away.

Suddenly a wild expression came rushing onto his face, and in a flash he sprang up and got hold of a sickle. He brandished the weapon with full vigour aiming at his wife's neck. Since she dodged in the nick of time, the sickle went past hissing like a snake, missing her neck only by a whisker. While trying to dodge, she lost her balance and landed on the floor. In an instant, despite the fall, she crawled towards her son and made a shield before him with her body. Her husband came forward with swaying steps, daggers in his gaze, and weapon in the hand.

She tried to shield her son from harm till the last minute. Yohannan screamed wildly in fear, and she desperately cried and prayed for the intervention of God. He moved forward with unsteady steps and raised the weapon, totally disregarding the screams and tears of his wife and son. The next moment, it would swoop down with a swish. Yohannan closed his eyes involuntarily, the desperate prayers of the mother reached its zenith; within a few seconds it would be silenced forever.

Suddenly powerful winds howled and engulfed the hut, pushing the door open violently. Under its impact, the father gave a start and turned around. An object akin to a flame was glowing at the entrance, with a radiance which gradually overpowered the dimness and illuminated the household. The man in the murderous mindset, dazzled by the flame, lost his bearings and slammed onto the floor. The anguished wail of the mother stopped in an instant. All remained thunderstruck and powerless, even to move. Gradually the flame started assuming human form and turned into a girl of celestial grace. At first, Yohannan assumed that it was none other than Our Lady, and her radiance took over the surroundings.

The father struggled to raise his head to gaze at the visitor on account of the intense brightness of the apparition, and like a kitten with unpeeled eyes, he wriggled on the floor. As a flame spinning in the breeze, the apparition turned around, gliding her hand gently and beckoning them to follow. The man sprang up in bewilderment, and it seemed he was no longer out of his senses. He gathered his family and started following her like an obedient child.

The darkness unfolded its blanket over the heights and cast it wide. As if in hallucination, they followed the halo without faltering and proceeded through the uneven mountainous terrain. Yohannan held his mother's hand, firmly. Those poor souls were totally unaware of where they were heading. Like very docile children they followed the light without questioning the logic of their action.

The recollection of golden hair, the long loose outfit cascading in

44

the breeze, remained fresh in the mind of Yohannan, as if leaving an everlasting imprint. The fear and uncertainty which had coiled on the household like a highly venomous snake started easing off. A few minutes back, they were devoid of hope, but now they entertained a gleam of optimism; there was not an iota of despair . . . instead, the intense desire to carry on kept their spirits buoyant.

Somewhere along the journey, the radiance turned and smiled at Yohannan. It appeared like the descent of the moon on to the heights, and the grace in that smile was enough to lead one towards the Almighty, throughout one's life.

In the thickening darkness, in the early hours of the night, under the strict guidance of the radiance, they negotiated the mountainous terrain with firm steps, and the journey culminated in a mansion, on top of a hillock, blazing with flowers even at night. They were welcomed into the household by Tresa's parents. That night, that moment, the fate of Yohannan's family was reordered. His parents found employment in the plantations of Tresa's father. With great relief, they enjoyed the love of the ideal host and slept peacefully that night, under Tresa's roof.

The next morning, just before returning, the family received a precious and invaluable gift from Tresa. It was a beautiful Bible in English, leather bound, bearing golden letters and a red lace.

Yohannan paused for a while. The light breeze begot many light ripples on the lake, and the cloud flakes scudded through the wind to scrape themselves against the peaks.

'That day I realized the existence of a great truth . . . there is a God who answers the cries of broken hearts,' in a confident voice Yohannan said, beaming with optimism.

'I still treasure the Bible given us by Tresa . . . but I cannot read English . . . cannot read it . . . I am not educated enough to read and comprehend the meaning . . . still, I treasure it.' It was evident that Yohannan was overwhelmed by powerful emotions.

'Who prompted her to travel through dangerous mountainous paths that night? Who is the one who brought her to our hut in the nick of time? I have no doubts . . . it is none other than the Almighty God.'

Yohannan was not merely communicating—he was proclaiming a great truth to the peaks, forests, to the reservoir and to every blade of grass, at the top of his voice.

'The Lord who created the earth . . . the Lord who created the universe.' He threw a question at me about what would have been the outcome had it not been for the timely intervention of Tresa, and the thought of it sent a chill through my spine. Yohannan added, 'That day I made up my mind to dedicate my life to the God who had saved my family from horrible disaster . . . that is how I became a missionary.'

He continued, 'Brother, I am unattractive in terms of appearance . . . not desirable in terms of skills . . . not outstanding in terms of communication . . . but I am submitting my humble resources to the Lord . . . I continually traverse mountains and forests to console the sorrowful, to scatter the pearls, rubies and diamonds of the gospel. With the guidance of God, I was able to save many farming households—many of these people were on the verge of suicide . . . this life as the servant of the Almighty is the greatest gift from him.'

'I will again scatter gifts among the deprived . . . I will challenge the mountains, forests and the wild to proclaim the word of God . . . I will fight for God till my last breath.'

The lofty mountains echoed the proclamations of Yohannan. Under its impact, the ripples on the lake stopped for a second, and the wind came to a halt. The forests, tea gardens and the greens stood still in ecstasy as if listening to the Gospel.

8

We opened the food packets when the sun was overhead and enjoyed the culinary skills of Esteppan. While eating, I made an allusion to the woman who had taken over the cave. Surprisingly, Yohannan responded to my remarks with an emotional outburst.

'She is the Queen of Prostitutes mentioned in the Book of Revelations,' he said when I told him how she had appeared before me and disappeared immediately.

'The devil is extremely scared of the cross, likewise she is scared since you are from the church . . . she is bound to stay away from you.' He did not agree when I said that it would not have been possible for her to have known my association with the church.

'She is as sharp as a needle. She knows where to hit and when to hit . . . at times her devilish eyes reflect lust, at times they reflect fiery temper. She is as voracious as a dragon and wants to swallow everything she sees . . . let me complete the tasks at hand . . . I will see to it that she is driven out of this place.'

His remarks were suffused with intense hatred for the cave-dweller.

'She is sinful to the hilt, she deserves eternal fire.' With these strong words, he put a stop to the matter. After eating, we reclined on the green and enjoyed the soothing breeze laden with the moisture of the reservoir. On the other side of the lake herds of elephant, deer and bison were visible.

Cleverly, I diverted the topic to the enigma of Tresa. Yohannan gave me a detailed account of their ancestral home which is no longer occupied. The house is under the supervision of the couple Augustin and Veronica who served the family of Tresa over many decades. Joshua, the son of Augustin and Veronica, is in charge of the upkeep of the mansion. Yohannan concluded by remarking that Joshua does an excellent job of maintaining the ancestral home. It was Veronica who had nursed Tresa since her birth, like a mother.

There was a slight pause in the conversation. The cloud flakes drifting through the air appreciably dimmed the sunlight.

'Yohannan, what is happening in the heights . . . have there been any reported sightings of Tresa after her death?' I asked the most vexing question.

All of a sudden uneasiness showed on his face.

'Some incidents have been reported. The heights are under the grip of fear . . . people are staying at home after evening.'

The ripples went on increasing in the reservoir and the breeze kept on gaining momentum. Suddenly there was a roar which lasted for a few moments above the summit of the peaks. We raised our eyes to the sky anxiously.

Thick black clouds were accumulating near the summit, and the reservoir began to turn dark reflecting the changes in the sky. The thought of the destructive power of the lightning accompanying the clouds sent a harpoon through my heart.

'It may rain . . . let us go.' Yohannan leapt up, we quickly got ready for the return journey. With hasty steps, we headed for the forests, and the sunlight kept on weakening steadily with the expansion of the cloud cover. Just before entering the forest, I turned back and cast a glance at the scenario behind us. The intensifying wind threw the seeds of darkness all over the sky vigorously, and the sun was almost eclipsed under the cloud cover. We waded through the forest in poor light. It was drizzling when we came out of the woods; we parted and proceeded in different directions with an agreement to meet again.

I came in the vicinity of the cave on my way back to the vicarage, and found its mouth was still covered with a sackcloth, and through the semi-transparency of the sackcloth appeared the gleam of a flame. The drizzle turned to shower, and I darted like a horse towards the vicarage. The moment I reached the vicarage, the doors of heaven collapsed bursting the cloud cover, and the retreating monsoon slammed onto the heights.

The vicar, who appeared to be in high spirits, welcomed me back. It was evident that he had broken through the wall of troubles by dint of prayer. The sight of the beaming vicar bolstered my confidence, and after a powerful prayer, we all sat down for dinner.

The vicar reminded me of the Holy Communion Service scheduled on the next day. He asked me to assist him at the altar throughout the service, and I accepted wholeheartedly. Then he entrusted me with the most difficult task of giving the sermon to the large congregation since he felt his voice could not stand the strain of service and sermon together on the same day. I accepted both the commands with open arms. Then the vicar wished me sound sleep and proceeded with soft steps to the bedroom chanting Psalm No 121.

'I look up to the mountains . . . does my help come from there?

My help comes from the Lord, who made heaven and earth

He will not let you stumble . . . the one who watches over you will not slumber.'

The beautiful verses of the psalm carrying the message of God's care and protection came drifting though the air.

'The Lord keeps you from all harm and watches over your life

The lord keeps watch over you as you come and go both now and forever.'

The voice of the vicar thinned out gradually. The message conveyed through the verses of the psalm held great significance that evening; neither thorn nor stone pierced my feet throughout the journey through the dense forest. We remained safe under the shield of the Almighty and the realization of the fact increased my confidence tenfold.

Next morning . . . only twenty-four more days to Christmas. A huge turnout of people from all walks of life reached the church at the break of dawn for the service. Together, they toiled and festooned the church complex. The crib and the manger were moulded into shape, star lights were pieced together, and they polished the lamps for illumination. For the next thirty-two days, the church complex was going to be clothed in the elegance of Christmas illumination. This time-honoured practice fills every nook and corner of the heights with the festive atmosphere.

The service commenced with the reading of lessons, and the voice of the vicar echoed through the interiors of the church in the form of Gregorian chant. I was amazed at the powerful voice coming from the aged and worn out vocal cords: it sounded like the roar of a lion. The vicar had always been a youngster at the altar where he appears like a person who is untouched by time; his chanting seemed to storm the gates of heaven, and the metallic rhythm of the oscillating incense holder turned out to be an accompaniment to the chanting.

The eddy of smoke emitted by the incense holder carried the fragrance of divinity, which saturated and purified the air. Through their golden voices, the choir betook the congregation to celestial bliss, and the service turned out to be a pleasant experience, elevating my heart to the highest levels of spirituality. The congregation appeared like a self-resurrecting phoenix, getting rid of the sinful past.

Then arrived the opportunity for delivering the task entrusted to me; with a sturdy determination I took the lectern and unfolded the scriptures. Then, I made eye contact with the congregation. All eyes were focused on me. The church was fully packed with all kinds of people: children, women, adults, the elderly, the rich, the poor, the healthy and the unhealthy. Suddenly I came under the possession of a divine force which compensated my weaknesses when it came to public speaking. I shared that part of the scripture which I had medi-tated over a couple of days back, and the message of finding the Almighty in the deprived was communicated with vigour and power. It seemed my tongue launched the message from the scriptures in the form of sparks. The congregation were all ears. I ruthlessly launched fiery arrows at the laziness, selfishness and avarice of the world. While delivering the sermon, my glance accidentally landed on the bushes, which stood a little away from the church, swaying in the wind. I saw something strange, totally unexpected, through the gaps formed by the violent tottering of the leaves and branches. Since the sight pierced my heart with a sword, I faltered and fumbled which disrupted the rhythm of the sermon. The congregation cast glances at one another, and the vicar raised his head anxiously. In a flash, I regained my presence of mind and the rhythm of the sermon, and proclaimed the word of God, fluently, without interruption.

After the service, I turned into a mere islet amidst hundreds of members in the congregation who came forward to introduce themselves to me. They all thanked me for the message which had touched their hearts. While talking to the believers, I cast glances to the bushes and tried to confirm in vain what I had witnessed a few moments back. I even doubted the reliability of my eyes.

In the afternoon, the heights became enveloped in a thin veil of mist. I fortified myself with another layer of warm clothes as he chill grew sharp. This is the month in which winter is at its coldest.

Despite the intense cold, a large section of the congregation turned up in the evening to witness the lighting of the lamps which marks the beginning of the advent. December first is a day of great significance for the parish since this is the day the lamps are lighted officially. Till the next month, at night, the church complex and its vicinity would be flooded with the radiance of illumination.

We reached the vicarage late at night after the celebrations and prayers. That night I struggled to find sleep. The vicar and the inhabitants of the vicarage were in deep sleep owing to the physical exertions the celebrations had occasioned. My mind remained turbulent and I kept on turning from side to side on the bed. The whisper of a shower was audible faintly. The jarring screech of a wild bird came from afar. With an uneasy heart, I stared into the darkness.

9

On account of an insatiable craving to visit the mansion that used to be the official residence of my father, I set off with Devassy on a crisp morning. The house carrying the tag 'The Colonial Marvel' was located on the topmost point of the loftiest hill in the heights. The mansion, dating back to the era of the British Raj, had really been a marvel of stone and timber, and had extensive grounds with orchards and gardens. The guidance and presence of Devassy turned out invaluable as I racked my brain in vain to retrieve the illegible sense of direction from the past, a decade and half.

Invigorated by the fresh air and the aroma of luxuriant greenery, we negotiated the undulations of the landscape with nimble feet. Walking on the undulating terrain I often felt like floating on a sudden gush of flash flood, peaking, pitching and snaking through the mountains. With pronounced impatience, I tried to spot the colonial marvel in the maze of luxuriant vegetation.

Suddenly the footsteps of Devassy came to a halt bringing my energetic strides to an abrupt end.

'There it is.' He pointed upwards as if targeting an avian, and I threw my glance towards the direction he pointed and found the elegant mansion on top of the highest peak in the vicinity. The long and winding driveway coming from the front yard and finishing at the bottom of the hill appeared like a python of remarkable length meandering down the slopes through thick vegetation.

I stood still for a few moments with my eyes fastened on the mansion that had been my home during my childhood. Against the backdrop of scudding cloud flakes across the sky, the once official residence of my father put on an element of mystery. With steady steps and casting short glances towards the steep hill, we proceeded farther and started negotiating the steep ungravelled driveway.

As we rattled along the long, winding and steep driveway, like a blushing maiden the mansion on top of the hill hid her face behind the slopes and played hide and seek with our progress through the twists and turns of the path. As we progressed the tea shrubs gave way to fruit trees and were eventually replaced by trees laden with beautiful flowers. The very sight of blazing flowers brought back vivid recollections from my childhood about indulging in gardening as a child under the supervision of my mother. I recalled sliding down the driveway like a river bursting its banks and also that these misadventures came to an abrupt end one day when the ground was extremely slippery on account of overnight rain and I fell. I still carry the mark of the long gash on my right leg as if imprinted with the political map of Kerala.

We climbed upward along the slope of the driveway edged with the garden blazing with bright flowers. As we negotiated the final sharp turn the architectural marvel concealed her face once again behind the profusion of flowers. With great enthusiasm and vigour we strode through the last few yards of the driveway, and all of a sudden out of nothing appeared the house in its fullest glory. The Colonial Marvel reappeared as elegant as ever, absolutely untouched by time. The glass windows, tiled sloping roof and the pot plants edging the perimeter of the structure appeared to be a tiny corner on the face of the earth not ravaged by time. Finally we stepped on to the well-gravelled front yard of the mansion.

The golden trumpet in full bloom snaking up to the roof of the portico covered the structure with gold and gave the mansion the appearance of a king with a golden crown. The half wall bordering the front yard appeared intact and the silver oak with outstretched branches looked inviting and unassuming.

'The house is lying vacant at the moment, awaiting the next official to come in,' said Devassy.

'Devassy . . . is it possible to have a look inside?' I expressed my desire to see once again the interiors of the mansion that had witnessed my deeds, misdeeds and pranks as a child.

'Let me have a word with the watchman . . . he stays at the rear of the mansion.' Devassy proceeded to explore the possibility of getting in so that I could explore the elegant interiors.

Standing on top of the lofty hill near the facade of my one-time dwelling, I turned back, casting my eyes far and wide. Right before me, nature unravelled the kaleidoscope of the divine immersing me in the influence of pulsating emotions. I stood face to face with the fort-like cloud-capped ranges of the Western Ghats, and the tea gardens on the slopes assumed the appearance of an undulating green carpet rolled out over the landscape. In the cool, gentle breeze the cloud flakes drifted around me like fairies.

This is where I stood in awe, years ago, watching the elegant progress of the south west monsoon clouds. The thick mass of clouds marching on to the Western Ghats resembles a huge herd of elephants. The destructiveness of the north east monsoon used to shake me to the core, and I used to stand in utter amazement at the sight of the mist getting folded and unfolded around the tender fingertips of the gentle breeze.

This is where the foundation of my spirituality took deep root. Seated on the half wall bordering the front yard, under the shade of the silver oak, I listened with all ears to the tales my mother told me based on the scriptures. In the salubrious warmth of the forenoon sun she unveiled before me, in her own words, the immense phenomenon of creation mentioned in the Book of Genesis. With gaping mouth and bated breath I virtually witnessed the conception of the heavens and the earth. My eyes remained dazzled for minutes under the first encounter with the light created by God. I saw with my own eyes the accumulation of water paving the way for the creation of dry land and the oceans. Like a silent observer I witnessed the sprouting of plants, blooming of flowers and growth of vegetation painting the landscape green. My senses stood testimony to the proliferation of the terrestrials on the land and the avians in the air.

On another cold forenoon I wandered through the antediluvian landscape holding my mother's hand. With a pounding heart I witnessed the doors of heaven collapsing and the thick sheet of water inundating the entire world tossing the arc of Noah with giant waves. My ears almost turned deaf at the undefinable roar of the oceans. This is the corner where I came to know about the Hebrew boy who was drawn from the Nile by the daughter of the Pharaoh who named him Moses. With heightened fear I witnessed the parting of the Red Sea and associated the thinning out of barren clouds in the heights with this event.

I associated the fury of the north west monsoon with the restoration of the Red Sea and considered the trees uprooted in the turbulence as the chariots of Pharaoh that were shattered by the restoration of the great water.

I was thrilled and leapt at the triumph of little David over Goliath and standing on the very spot, hurling the catapult bought from the weekly bazaar, challenged the mighty ranges of the Ghats, identifying myself with the shepherd boy. This is where I was introduced to the miracle-working hands of Jesus and I stood in awe fully dazzled by the intensity of his halo. I cried at his sufferings on the cross and rejoiced in the good news of his resurrection.

Hanging on to the fingers of my mother, hanging on to the tip of her sari, I walked through the land of Canaan, saw the Sea of Galilee and scaled the towering heights of Mt Sinai. Through her overwhelming narratives I enjoyed the sweetness of the Grapes of Canaan, tasted the acridness of the Olives and marvelled at the Cedars of Lebanon.

During those beautiful and eventful days, I was fortunate enough to embark on another journey through the landscape of ancient India. In the pleasant afternoons during the weekends, inhaling the air laced with the aroma of tea powder, my father led me to the colourful world of the epics.

Licking my tender fingers coated with butter and cream, I enjoyed the taste of the purest of the pure with infant Krishna, and explored the banks of River Kalindi, jostling shoulders with him. Like churning milk in a wooden churn, he churned out the most melodious music for me on his flute.

With a fluttering heart, I tread through the battlefields of the Mahabharata and looked at the greatest war in the history of mankind. I marvelled at the archery skills of Arjuna and shuddered under the thunderous vibrations of the string of his celestial bow. I wept profusely when the towering figure of Bheeshma collapsed under a barrage of arrows.

I witnessed the nocturnal battle between Karna and Khadorgaja and even went up to the extent of associating the ranges of the Western Ghats and the thunderous clouds of the retreating monsoon with them. In the height of obsession I fashioned a bow with cane and attached a jungle vine to it as string. Adorned with the bow and a quiver filled with arrows I tried to emulate Lord Rama himself. For the restoration of peace and justice on earth, I fiercely launched arrows hither and thither from the vicinity of Colonial Marvel, sitting on top of the hill.

One afternoon, adorned with bow and quiver, I strolled through the woods in the backyard of Colonial Marvel. Unknowingly and unthinkingly my mind associated itself with Rama, the prince of Ayodhya. In the slanting golden rays of the sun the woods appeared like the forest on the banks of River Sarayu where the giantess Tadaka prowled. I stood near the precipice at the edge of the woods, and with awe viewed the canopy of forests sloping downwards along the deep declivity. I considered myself as the prince of Ayodhya, and took utmost pride in the identification. I became aware of my impending mission—'the slaughter of Tadaka', and with boundless vigour raised the bow against the sky; a wind appeared out of nowhere and lashed ruthlessly. I remained a few moments with the bow upraised; the wind kept on intensifying, and I felt the throb of nature within me. It was a hair-raising experience and seemed to last forever.

From the corner of the eyes, I witnessed the gathering of clouds as if churned by the wind, weakening the sunlight considerably. As if challenging the demon, I stretched the string of the bow taut and released the string to sound the battle cry. I stood frozen under the impact of a thunder, and even felt the woods resonate to its terrific impact.

Then to my utter amazement, the clouds gathered in the sky took irregular patterns; in one instant they appeared in the form of huge boulders and turned into the shape of huge granite pillars in the next instant. The wind kept on gaining momentum, evoking in me the feeling of the gust of air belched from the dreadful mouth of the demon Tadaka. Streaks of lightening appeared, reappeared and snaked through the sky, the woods swayed violently triggering a barrage of twigs and dry leaves from the forest floor. I remained thunderstruck and tried to shield my eyes from the falling leaves and twigs driven by the wind. I heard a strange dreadful noise in the sky under which the entire place shivered and shuddered, and with intense fear I uncovered my eyes to view the emotions playing out in the sky.

A cloud of immense size caught my attention and surprisingly it appeared heading towards me, expanding every moment, and seemed to be conquering the entire length and breadth of the sky through its phenomenal expansion. Steadily it took the shape of something akin to a human—hands and legs of gigantic proportions protruded out, followed by the formation of a face, ugliest of the ugly. Her tongue lolled out, hands remained extended like the wings of a huge bird, and with protruding teeth, like a huge mountain she came hurtling towards me. The winds intensified, the ground shuddered, and I struggled hard to control the shaking of my hands. I pulled an arrow from the quiver and fixed it on the bow, pulled the string strug- gling to control the shaking fingers. The fearful apparition reached gigantic proportions and appeared to extend to the four corners of the sky. The free fall of the demon continued and it looked determined to pulverise me through a blow from its nostrils. Involuntarily I released the arrow; the string returned to its normal position with a jerk and remained fluttering for a few moments.

My eyes were dazzled by a powerful lightning; close on its heels arrived a thunder and the four corners of the earth shuddered under the blow that made me numb. The powerful bolt from the sky brought my mother out, and she came hurtling through the woods, then embraced me, imparting a feeling of security as if I were embraced by the divine. In an instant the wind subsided; the dust, twigs and dry leaves settled down, the woods regained tranquillity, and the clouds in the sky melted away instantaneously. Through the diluting cover of vapour the sky regained its azure hue and the sun reappeared.

The incident still remains as an enigma in my mind—was it really nature's response to my innocent gesture to restore good over evil, or was it a mere hallucination of a boy overly obsessed by the epics?

The deep roots of the Hindu religion in my heart met with questions coated with scepticism from many in the family. My father wanted to groom me as an Indian who is passionate about the nation irrespective of the faith.

Slowly, I moved to the shade of the silver oak which had been a silent eavesdropper to the myriad of tales from the Bible and the Indian epics. If it could speak, like a skilled storyteller the tree would have been recounting the beauty of the tales deeply engraved in its growth rings over a period of five years. The branches of the silver oak fluttered in the gentle breeze; in the distance the vanishing haze brought out the majestic ranges of Western Ghats in all their elegance. The landscape became dotted with the figures of the labourers in the tea garden, and with the baskets on their back, they all looked like a novel version of marsupials.

I turned back at the sound of footsteps and found the elderly watchman dressed in khaki accompanying Devassy. He appeared healthy in the outfit and headgear that can withstand the challenges of winter, and despite my entreaties he remained insistent on kneeling before me and kissing my hands as if greeting the pontiff. As if bestowed with a major privilege, in buoyant spirits he moved towards the facade and unlocked the door, the bunch of keys he carried clanging all the time.

Standing at the threshold of the facade, I turned in casting glances towards the extensive gravelled front yard. This was the exact spot where I was ushered by my parents into the world of giving and sharing; they inculcated in me a deep passion for charity. This was where I received advice from my parents about sharing resources with the deprived, and the vivid recollection of giving away clothes, food and other things came rushing to my mind. The faces of the recipients lit up in joy turned out to be a motivator for me to give more and more.

With the permission of the watchman, I stepped into the well-carpeted interiors and was amazed at the elegance of furniture and fixture that had remained in excellent condition even after the lapse of many years. The Colonial Marvel was well set to receive the new inhabitant who would have the authority over the entire district of hills and peaks. The elegant flight of winding stairs appeared before me lined with cylindrical banisters made of wood and I made my way upwards, with careful steps, through the carpeted stairs. As I climbed up, the base of the second floor appeared to be lowering itself slowly as if gliding down through the air. With heightened curiosity I stepped into all the five bedrooms on the first floor and spent a few moments there.

During our occupancy of the mansion, we had never been short of visitors and guests except for a brief period when I was under the grip of a serious contagious illness. This is where I learned to throw the doors of my house open to the children of God from all walks of life, irrespective of caste, creed and religion. This is how I was shown how to travel an extra mile for the comfort of our brethren even at the cost of our own comfort. My parents found it blissful to earmark their time, set apart the resources and cut down on their own comfort for the sake of others, at times sowing the seeds of envy in the mind of the child in me. I despised the idea of sharing the time and resources with others that should have been devoted entirely for me, but was reluctant to air the bubbling displeasure and discontent.

I descended to the first floor through the winding stairs, reached the living room well furnished with elegant furniture, came near the large dining table at the end of the living room, and sat down near the table drawing a chair decorated with woodwork. It had been on this very spot I had witnessed the process of giving in abundance, in other words the act of giving from the heart without the constraints of arithmetic calculations. The recollection of that day is still vivid in my mind—a young boy had turned up before the facade with unkempt hair and tattered garments, his eyes were tearful, and he appeared frail on account of severe and prolonged starvation. His humble pleadings sounded like the bleating of a goat to my ears to which I responded with a giggle, but his cries, triggered by the ruthless pangs of hunger, melted the gentle heart of my mother instantly.

As expected, the doors opened to his cries, and with immense curiosity I watched how the host honoured the youngster at the table. With a ladle she served rice grains as white as pearls onto the concave plate, then evened out the surface with the bottom of the ladle, again served rice on top, and filled it to capacity. A few minutes later appeared the dish filled with the grain with curry on top like an icing on a cake. With bated breath I watched the movements of the starved youngster when he scooped up rice ball after rice ball. His jaws worked like a high-speed machine. The fingers, palms, hands and mouth too worked together like a perfectly automated machine, and he continued scooping, chewing and swallowing the food without pause, seemingly forgetting even the process of breathing in and out. For the first time in my life I realized how excruciating and painful is the state of being deprived of food, and the image of the youngster looking at my mother, after having eaten, with tearful eyes as if beholding a goddess got registered in my heart permanently.

Following the swift flow of the stream of memories I proceeded to the spacious master bedroom on the ground floor, and the doors opened with a prolonged moan at the gentle force my hands exerted. Before my eyes appeared the spacious floors carpeted with coir; with hesitant feet I stepped into the room. In the room overflowing with elegance time appeared to be standing still; the clock had stopped a decade and a half ago.

I sat on the huge bed made of excellent wood. This was the room that had witnessed the most crucial moments of my life; it was in this room that I learnt beyond doubt that prayer has power and the presence of the Almighty, though invisible, is everywhere, and that He responded to the heartbreaking wails of human beings. In the sunlight filtering in through the translucent curtains I sat recollecting the events from the past that have left permanent impressions on my life.

10

I struggled and wriggled under the excruciating pain of thousands of needles piercing my skin. Like a wilted stem of pepperomia, I was extremely weakened, and any effort to swallow felt like gulping hot and liquefied lava down the throat. Poxes that were as large as gooseberries disfigured my body and each one felt like a sharp nail piercing the flesh and chipping at the bones. The stress of the dreadful disease outweighed fully the endurance of a mere twelve-year old boy.

My parents were in low spirits, and many visitors who used to frequent our home were scared away by the contagious nature of the illness. People were scared off if even my name was mentioned at the time.

I caught the illness when my family was about to relocate to the capital city. It started with mild symptoms of weariness and fever, and on the following day poxes started surfacing on the body, with the fever intensifying. Because of the effect of the disease, I frequently slipped into unconsciousness. My parents were always near my bed, round the clock. Both prayers and medicines turned ineffective and my health deteriorated day by day.

Even in the height of illness I could see like a smudged paint the image of my mother praying to God tearfully, and dad struggling to gulp back tears. I was heading for a mysterious black hole and the realization of this fact induced fear in my parents.

Decades back the disease which had gripped me used to frighten people with its history of wiping off whole villages. But then, the disease itself was on the verge being wiped off from the face of the earth, when it came crashing down on me like a curse.

I remained at death's door for nearly a fortnight, and on the fourteenth day medical science too abandoned me, driving harpoons into the hearts of my parents. The doctors passed their professional verdict, calling for a miracle of all times. My parents tearfully pleaded the Almighty for that 'miracle of all times.'

I remained oscillating between the realms of unconsciousness and semi-consciousness. During times of semi-consciousness, I vaguely witnessed the tears and prayers of my parents. On the fourteenth day, I almost lost my consciousness leaving vague memories of the Bible being read and desperate prayers mixed with sobs. I remained in serious condition for the next two days; in other words, I was under the gravitational pull towards the black hole of death.

Under the pull of the black hole, my free fall into the abyss of darkness commenced, and with increasing velocity every second I plunged into the darkest depths of non-existence. Suddenly a gleam of light appeared afar. The tiny gleam kept on expanding and intensifying every moment. Involuntarily, my body responded to a soothing divine touch which evoked the feeling of a short, abrupt stream of electric current passing through my body. My arms and legs thrust forth under its impact, and I underwent an experience of levitation and weightlessness. Then I experienced the feeling of being lowered onto a flowerbed and getting bandaged by floral garlands. The excruciating pain eased off considerably. Somebody touched my head and ran fingers through my hair and it turned out to be a pleasant experience. I enjoyed the rare feeling of being sprinkled with rose-water, my eardrums responded to the melody of celestial music, and I found comfort in the divinely pleasant experience. Then, the gleam of light that assumed the shape of a flame drifted away gradually; the farther it went the more it assumed the shape of a human, and vanished like a speck.

Finally the 'miracle of all times' alluded to by the medical fraternity turned into reality. Staging a comeback from an almost impossible situation, I broke the shackles of the deadly disease. To be precise, the hand of the Almighty plucked me out of the clutches of death and replanted me in the province of the living. The pain eased off, and the poxes shrunk. When I regained consciousness I found my parents thanking the Almighty, in tears. The visions I encountered at the peak of the illness continued to be enigmatic till I received from my mother, after relocating to the capital city, a detailed account of the events that had taken place.

For two days after being abandoned by medical science I remained unconscious, and my condition deteriorated in the evening of the second day. Blood pressure and pulse rate plummeted to alarming levels. My parents cried to God through fervent prayers, there was darkness all over the room, and the lean flame of the lantern was totally unable to combat the thick blanket of darkness. Suddenly, a radiance appeared at the door, and gradually assumed a human shape. It took a few moments for my parents, who were in the abyss of grief, to realize the presence of Tresa. Her face bespoke severe grief and eyes looked unusually dull and sorrowful. She came close to me (according to my mother drifted towards me) with measured steps and humble carriage. My parents did their best to hinder her by highlighting the deadliness of the disease but she remained steadfast; heedless of the warnings she sat beside me, and touched my body mottled with repulsive scars and wounds. Turning a deaf ear to the pleadings of my parents, turning a blind eye to her own safety, she embraced me, and lifted and placed my head onto her lap. Like skimming cream, she wiped off the pus and scab from my face, then pressed her soft palms on my head, raised her eyes to heaven and prayed. The waves of the prayer drifted through the air and echoed upon the walls of the room. She sprinkled my body with tears and kissed my forehead after her prayer.

'Fear not.' She bade adieu after chanting these words to my parents, and I witnessed her disappear with eyes half-open. She appeared like a flame drifting away and finally disappeared as a speck of light. That was the last I saw of Tresa.

My health showed signs of improvement, blood pressure and pulse rate regained normalcy within a few hours. Next morning the fever subsided leaving me profusely sweating, the poxes and wounds healed as if cauterized. Within a few days, I recouped completely, much to the amazement of the medical fraternity.

That night a new wave of howling of wolves surfaced from the forests, and the dogs of the heights played perfect accompaniment to this horrifying music of death, as if a nocturnal evil power was taking possession of the heights. My heart throbbed severely, and I shivered and sweated under fear. Then came to my rescue Psalm 121 chanted by the vicar, a few hours back, and the verses started to rise from the bottom of my heart, and the fear began to ease. I surrendered everything to the Almighty, and gradually unshackled myself from the grip of fear.

Next day I was greeted by the morning, almost frozen under the extreme weather. Heedless of the severity of winter, I set out for my morning stroll. I strengthened my defence against the chill by putting on another layer of shawl. Giving assurances of my return before breakfast I bade adieu to all in the vicarage.

Despite the sudden withdrawal of thick fog, the wind knifed me sharply. I proceeded to the tea gardens, moving parallel to the church complex. The divine fragrance that encircled me in the wind symbolized the invincibility of the creeper even at the height of winter. The rarest plant is thriving, outlasting the challenges of nature, and emitting heavenly fragrance much to the relief of pain-stricken souls.

A great energy kept on flowing, pulsating in the cells with vigour, and the divine fragrance of the creeper acted as a catalyst to this process. I proceeded with firm steps beaming with energy and confidence.

The tea gardens stood shivering in the chill. Crossing the narrow network of paths intersecting the tea gardens, I was about to negotiate the slippery surface of the cluster of rocks. Suddenly, there came from the openings amongst the rocks, two images in the form of human beings. They were none other than the 'Queen of Prostitutes' and 'the son' (in Yohannan's description) and accidentally they landed up right under my nose. At my sight, she gave a violent start and with fearful glances at regular intervals tried to hide herself behind the rocks. Her son was as weary and thin as a twig, and both of them were dressed in rags totally insufficient to tackle the cold winter. It was evident that both of them were in deep distress.

Then arrived the chilling wind with poignant edges and I wriggled under its needling effect. 'The Whore' desperately tried to save her son from the chill by pressing him firmly to her bosom, and it turned out to be an effort in vain to provide the struggling child with some of her own warmth. Her eyes were indicative of her intense concern for the child. I became totally oblivious of filthy tag 'The Queen of Prostitutes' and considered her as my own 'sister' who was struggling in acute helplessness.

Suddenly I heard the roaring of a mighty storm from heaven as mentioned in the Acts of the Apostles. Under the impact of the strange phenomenon, even the cluster of rocks shuddered. The tea shrubs in the vicinity went spinning like a top, and the strange phenomenon started to encircle us.

The shrubs amidst the cluster of rocks were trodden onto the ground under the pressure of the wind, and the next moment the strange phenomenon assumed a perfect circular shape. Like a demon-possessed woman, the vegetation danced with abandon. We were at the exact centre of the phenomenon. Even the blades of grass appeared to be plucked out of the ground by the strong wind.

All of a sudden, I felt the eye of the storm focusing on me, and felt being crushed under the pressure as if ten elephants were standing over my body. The powerful tentacles of the wind made me hamstrung, and it appeared that nature was desperate to communicate something. My garments fluttered violently; the shawl, the perfect defence against chill, appeared struggling to detach itself from me to balloon high up on its own accord. On account of its eagerness to fly away, it no longer appeared like an inanimate object. I tried my best to restrain the pranks of the shawl, to stay enveloped under its warmth. Finally I gave the object some room, and like a bird desperate to leave its cage, the shawl rocketed high, flattened out and remained in the air like a canopy for a few moments. In the next instant, the streams of air dragged the shawl in the direction of the cluster of rocks. Like a kite swooping on a chick, the 'Queen of Prostitutes' leapt in the air, snatched the shawl with the perfection of an acrobat and enveloped her child in its warmth.

The strange phenomenon ceased in the next instant and surviving the rage of convulsions, tea plants and other vegetation stood still. The 'Queen of Prostitutes' and her son snuggled close and found comfort under the warmth of the piece of cloth peeled off from me by nature. My loss turned out to be a gain for them, and provided a new lease of life for mother and child. I could read the sparks of gratitude in their eyes. I returned to the vicarage and turned back while climbing the stairs leading to the church. Even then, their eyes remained fixed on me.

I reached the vicarage and the loss of one of the shawls came to the attention of the vicar.

'Where is your shawl?' he asked with curiosity.

My answer was crisp, strong and clear: 'I have given it to the Almighty.'

11

At the heights, nature underwent a sea change in the afternoon. The chill turned sharper, the sky became overcast, and the blanket of fog that enveloped the heights prevented sunbeams from percolating onto the ground. Even well before evening, the heights came under the grip of thick darkness. I was scared even to peep through the window, at the ground which had a tint of terror.

The vicar, who was in high spirits, spoke volumes about the parish, and the ongoing missions in the vicinity of the heights. In the middle of the conversation I enquired about the incident which had compelled him to embark on an intense fasting prayer. He remained silent for a few minutes, and it appeared the question had dampened his enthusiasm. He assured me that it would be discussed in due course.

An uneasy silence crept into the room and vexed us to the core, and the embers in the fireplace hissed and spluttered. From afar came a rumbling, which lasted for a few minutes, and under its influence the window panes of the vicarage shuddered. The rumbling was akin to the noise which I heard at the reservoir two days before. It was evident that the retreating monsoon was all set to unleash another attack on the heights.

'This is very uncommon in the month of December,' the vicar commented on the rumbling of the thunder.

The vicar wanted to retire after dinner and he requested my presence in his room to share something of great significance.

I reached the bedroom that was half lit by the lantern, and the seriousness on the face of vicar stood out even in the dim light. I sat face to face with him with my curiosity spiralling high. Outside the vicarage, the wind growled and heralded the onset of another powerful rain, and the dazzle of lightning that appeared on the glass window sent harpoons through my heart.

'Child . . . a few minutes back . . . you asked me the reason for the fasting prayer.' The vicar spoke in a quivering voice. I nodded and sat attentively to hear more.

'Dear child . . . I have a problem,' said the vicar.

'What is it?' I asked.

The vicar remained silent for a few moments, pushing my curiosity to dizzying heights. Involuntarily I leaned forward fully focusing on him with ears sharpened.

'Tresa is my problem.'

The shudder originating in my heart radiated all over the body and my heart rate started spiralling upward. A powerful lightning flashed, a big crack of thunder followed and the entire vicarage stood aghast under its impact.

The narration of the vicar turned the clock back to a decade and half, to the month of November. The retreating monsoon slammed onto the heights with such intensity as was unknown in recorded history. Under its impact, the land shivered to the core, and streams overflowed for many weeks. Causing widespread damage, the rain continuously battered the high ranges forcing reservoirs to overspill.

On the last days of November, on an afternoon another thick blanket of clouds enveloped the heights and unleased its strength, all out, in the form of powerful rain. On that day, it was thick sheets of water and not mere raindrops which battered the heights.

The vicar gave a short respite to his narration, and used that short span of time to regulate his accelerating breath rate. He was being overwhelmed by powerful emotions. The rain kept on intensifying which produced the impression of the responsiveness of nature to tales of the past. The wind blew powerfully, and the noise of swaying branches acted as a barometer recording the fury of nature. After a while the breath rate of the vicar attained normalcy and he proceeded with the narration.

Throughout the day, the vicar endured a feeling of intense uneasiness and heaviness in his heart, which kept on intensifying every second. He proceeded to the prayer room, threw himself down before the crucifix and meditated intensely, growing unaware of the intensity of the rain which lasted many hours. His deep meditation was interrupted in the evening when one of the servants knocked on his door.

The servant announced the arrival of a group of visitors at the vicarage with a serious concern, and they were waiting on the ground floor to present their problem to the vicar. The vicar descended the flight of stairs from the first floor and found Tresa's father in a state of intense agitation.

They announced the heartbreaking news of the disappearance of Tresa since the last few hours. As usual, she went out in the forenoon for a stroll. The forenoon stroll had been a deep rooted habit of her's since she always found the mountains and landscape attractive. But contrary to the usual, she failed to return which made her father extremely worried about her safety in the wild weather. He, with the help of a team, scanned every nook and corner of the tea garden and the edges of the forest with a fine tooth comb which yielded no result. His labourers had been directed to the vicinity of the reservoir for a final search. An uneasy silence blanketed the interiors of the vicarage at the announcement of this news.

The vicar, who was rich in experience, stood frozen and spellbound. He really feared for the safety of this angel who had turned human, and prayed fervently for her protection. Every second of delay in tracing her could be fatal, and this realization drove the vicar into action. He sprang up and in a flash summoned enough motivation into the mentally shattered search team.

The vicar took over the reins of the search party, divided the team up into six units and despatched them to different directions. He took the lead of the sixth which consisted of Tresa's father, Augustine, and a few others. Despite battering rain and howling wind, the team embarked on their search. They fought against the poor visibility with cast-iron determination and waded forward, and with great difficulty, crossed the tea garden and headed for the cluster of rocks. Suddenly they encountered an unusual sight. In the poor light, a strange apparition was emerging from the gaps between the rocks and for a second, it was unclear whether it was human or not. It turned out to be something of short stature, and the vicar threw the glow of the lantern on it.

'My Lord,' responded that person.

Peeling off the enigma of darkness, the beams of the lantern brought out the identity of the person who was an aborigine youngster, short, dark and able bodied. He was in the traditional outfit with a headgear as protection against rain and was armed with a bow and a full quiver on his back. He called the vicar aside and whispered a few words in his ear, and at the instruction of the vicar the search party followed him.

Under the guidance of the nimble-footed youngster, they raced through the dense forest where sunlight is scanty even at noon. They realized the intensity of the rain on setting foot on the extensive grassland crossing the woods. The pattering of raindrops formed thousands of puddles. Following the guidance of the youngster they pushed through the drenched luxuriance of vegetation.

The vicar stopped for a while; in spite of the chill he sweated profusely. The turbulence in the form of heavy rain and strong wind went on without respite, accompanied by thunder and lightning. I understood the difficulties they all underwent that ill-fated evening.

The vicar recouped his lost energy and prepared to take me through the rest of the narrative.

Slowly and steadily they snaked through the fog, moisture and poor visibility. Every step appeared as lengthy as an epoch, and as they proceeded farther, the grassland turned more and more dense.

Suddenly, through the thin transparency of the mist came light beams. Their intensity kept on increasing with every step and eventually the beams of light turned themselves into flaming torches. Under a big tree stood an erected canopy, and under the canopy stood a group of armed aborigines who were on high alert as if guarding an invaluable diamond. With reluctance the vicar took a few paces forward and came across the sight which made him shudder, the effect of which was bound to last a lifetime.

Under the canopy the drenched body of a girl lay on the grass saturated with moisture. Jumping to some conclusion, Tresa's father screamed and burst into tears. The intensity of the tears and cries emerging from the shattered heart overpowered the battering of rain and crack of thunder. The vicar raised the lantern and directed the beam of light at the girl. She appeared like an angel, injured and fallen from the sky. The eyelids of that angelic face were closed, and her long hair and clothes were completely drenched. The deep cut on her lips stood out like a blot on the beautiful landscape.

The vicar raised her and carried her on his shoulders. To get medical help for Tresa two aborigine runners left like a flash towards the church. The vicar firmly believed in the existence of molecules of life in her motionless body. He darted like a wild horse carrying the body which was like a crushed rose, and the aborigines cleared the way for the vicar by chopping the dense vegetation down mercilessly.

The determination of the vicar to rekindle the molecules of life lying dormant in Tresa was as strong as a steel rope. Running along the grassland, traversing the dense forest and swimming against the strong current of the brook the team headed for the church in amazing pace. In the last leg of the journey the determined vicar showed the signs of breaking down, and Tresa's father took over the mission. Carrying his beautiful daughter, he headed for the church like an arrow released from a highly stretched bow.

At the command of the vicar, conveyed through the aborigines, the big doors of the church gave way that night, and the lamps were lit. The medical team came rushing to the church for the resuscitation of Tresa. Carrying his daughter on his shoulders Tresa's father came rushing into the church and placed her at the entrance. In a flash, the medical team encircled her and they desperately searched for the spark of life, and tried to rekindle it. Finally, they gave the final verdict and confirmed Tresa's death.

Suddenly, a streak of light came through the window and whizzed past us. With a loud explosion, the metallic objects in the room scattered in different directions. An ear-bursting thunder followed. For a second, I thought everything was over. But we survived, unscathed . . . how? . . . the hand of the Lord diverted the streak of lightning away from us . . . this is the only plausible explanation I can provide. The lightning which nearly missed us shook me to the core, and it took a few minutes for my heartbeat to return to normalcy. But the vicar encountered this event with utmost calm, without an iota of fear or frustrations on his face—instead, his face bore a tint of sorrow imprinted by the untimely loss of Tresa.

Tresa's father responded to the pronouncement of death like an insane; the walls of the church echoed with his screams. He lifted up her body and charged towards the altar. Laying her body on the altar he wept profusely.

The next day, in the evening under the overcast sky, her body was laid to rest. Every corner of the heights stood drenched in the tears of nature. The blades of grass, tea plants and the dense forests stood still as witnesses to the disaster. Then the heights went through uneasy and monotonous days in a row. For nearly a week the sky remained overcast and nature kept on weeping in the form of a drizzle. The thick blanket of fog which enveloped the heights drove the inhabitants to severe depression. The sunbeams remained reluctant to percolate to the land to usher in a gleam of hope in the valleys and grasslands. The heights remained so depressing.

'Nature literally wept,' the vicar sobbed, and I felt an excruciating pain in my heart, and on account of intense grief tear drops drew long channels on my face. The eerie silence again flooded the room, and the raindrops kept on battering the roof, and it appeared that nature herself was heartbroken at the recollection of the painful memories.

'How did she meet her end?' I asked when the overflowing emotions eased, and all of a sudden the vicar grew uneasy. In a flash, the rains intensified and like the shower of arrows launched by a huge army the raindrops slammed on the roof.

'Attacked by some wild animal,' he replied in a shaking voice, turning his face away from me; then he reclined on the bed. It was clear that the vicar was not mentally prepared for any further conversation. I rolled out the grass mat on the floor, flattened the blanket on it and stretched myself after lowering the flame of the lantern.

A terrifying series of thunder and lightning went past; every thunder and every lightning seemed determined to tear the heights to thousands of pieces. The presence of the saintly vicar kept fear out of my heart, but the sudden variations in the emotions of nature kept me in astonishment. I profoundly felt the desperate throbbing of nature to convey some mystery which is revealed only in part, and with a turbulent mind I kept rolling on the mat like a ship being tossed in the wind.

12

The next morning, the vicar came under the grip of acute physical uneasiness. Telling of Tresa's death had taken its toll. I tried to nurse him back to health and considered the opportunity of serving him as a great privilege. Since seeing 'the divine' in the ailing vicar, I enjoyed every moment of serving him and even perceived the bestowal of honours, as precious as diamonds, on me by the heavens.

In the afternoon, the vicar brought to my attention the coincidence of 33rd birthday of Tresa with that same day and this announcement took me by surprise. After her demise, Augustin and Veronica had started commemorating her birthday, every year. On this day the favourite fir tree of Tresa, which grows near the entrance of the ancestral home, gets decorated with festoons, ribbons and baubles, and the facade of the house basks in the radiance of hundreds of star lights. The ceremony always commences and concludes with the prayer of the vicar, and the time span between the commencement and the conclusion is strictly devoted to reading the scriptures, prayers, lighting of candles and the recapitulation of bright memories from the past. These arrangements have been going on for the past fifteen years, without fail.

That day, the absence of the vicar from the commemoration was almost certain, so he asked me to visit the ancestral home of Tresa that evening to lead the activities. With a fluttering heart, with prayers, I accepted the mission.

In the evening, after ablutions and prayers, I dressed in the traditional lily white and wrapped my chest with a thick shawl. Then I armed myself with that most powerful weapon, The Bible, bade adieu to the vicar and proceeded for the mission. The cart pre-arranged for my journey stood nearly a hundred metres away from the vicarage. In the poor visibility, its outline sowed the seeds of fear in me. The cart, which was as dark as darkness itself, had two horses to it; the lanterns fitted on each side gleamed faintly in the thin veil of the mist, and owing to the moisture coming from the snouts of the horses it appeared like an ugly steam engine.

Whinnying loudly, the horses trotted forward, clip-clopping in perfect harmony to the chime of bells, and came to a halt near me. The cart driver, clad in thick warm clothes, sat at the front. His efforts to avoid eye contact with me symbolized indifference and triggered ripples of fear in my mind. For a moment, I stood hesitant to step in but the very thought of the sanctity of the mission prompted me to move on, cleansing the fear from my mind. At last, I got into the cart with fervent prayers.

Suddenly the driver drew a thick curtain before me, and obscured the view fully. The horses neighed and galloped forward unsettling me with a powerful jerk, then the cart swayed violently and gained break-neck speed in a flash. It appeared that the cart was negotiating a steep downward slope after encircling the church complex. In the speeding cart I struggled to maintain balance and felt trapped in a vehicle that was on to a free fall to the depths of abyss. I cursed the moment of boarding the cart and tried to focus solely on God. After a while, it became evident that the cart was darting along a flat surface, having successfully negotiated the steep declivity. On account of the alarming velocity, the cart kept on swaying. I struggled to maintain balance and pulled back the curtain that obscured my view. The image of the moon appeared like an aerial ship which was on the decline and the vast expanse of tea gardens put on the appearance of a dark blanket. Thrown backwards at regular intervals, the silver oaks in the tea garden acted as a reliable gauge for measuring the lightning speed of the cart.

Alarmed by the momentum, involuntarily I pulled my hand away releasing the grip on the curtain flapping in the wind. I prayed fervently and after a while the cart showed signs of slowing down. The clopping of hoofs indicated a hard surface rolled. The cart was climbing an acclivity and finally came to a grinding halt. I stepped out, heaved a prolonged sigh of relief and right in front of me appeared the huge ancestral home of Tresa.

The facade was flooded with the radiance of many star lights and the fir-tree, the favourite of Tresa, stood like a Christmas tree dressed up before time. Pushing the front door open, I stepped into a room lit by candles and the glow of which was more than enough to bring out the elegance of the furniture and fixtures.

Suddenly the candlelight in the room started intensifying, the furniture, well-curtained windows and well-carpeted floor began standing out. The outline of the flight of stairs leading upwards and the railings kept on sharpening. I was dazzled by a flame oozing through the stairs and it started assuming human shape.

Somebody pulled me back from the past to the present. I came back to the golden glow of the candles and immediately recognized the aged Augustin who was standing near me. The next moment we both got interlocked in a firm embrace. He guided me to the large and elegant dining room which was also lit by candles. I recognized Veronica who was seated beside the dining table looking at me with a suppressed exuberance of joy. Then, in a snap, she rose up and almost choked me under a firm cuddle which was overflowing with motherly affection. I held her close to me, she leaned onto my chest, and I felt joyful when my bosom got soaked in her tears.

Augustine introduced his son 'Joshua' who was in charge of the maintenance of the ancestral home. I thanked him for his excellent stewardship, efficiency and diligence; the candle flames over the birthday cake marked the beginning of commemoration, and I unfolded the scriptures trusting the God to guide me to the ideal Bible passage which would be relevant in those circumstances. The Bible portion which revealed itself before me conveyed the prophecy about a divine infant.

The spirit of god will rest on him . . . He will give justice to the poor and make fair decisions for the exploited . . . He will wear right-eousness like a belt and truth like a garment . . . In that day the wolf and the lamp will live together . . . the leopard will lie down with the baby goat . . . The nations will rally to him and the land where he lives will be a glorious place.

After the rendition of the poetical verses of Isaiah, I prayed.

Immediately after the conclusion of the prayer came the fear-stricken neighing of the horses; close to its heels arrived a powerful wind which forced the doors open. The vivid shadows of the swaying pine trees appeared on the glass windows, and on the decorated fir tree chimed the bells with the twist and turns of the wind. The flames swayed and the candles on the birthday cake were put off by a sudden gust of air, as if blown out by someone invisible. We all were bewildered at the strange expressions of nature; the phenomenon lasted for a few seconds and died down. The chiming of the bells on the fir tree faded away gradually, and the swaying flames shone brightly, standing erect.

Veronica's expression changed. Her facial muscles stretched as if testing their tensile strength.

'Tresa . . . Tresa.' Shouting at the top of her voice, she sprang forward and rushed to the interiors of the house; it was evident that she was desperately searching for someone, and we followed her. After completing a futile search on the ground floor, like a lightning, she climbed to the first floor through the stairs overcoming the weak resistance offered by Augustine and Joshua. After another search in vain, she rushed downstairs like a landslide, and we foiled her attempt to traverse the front yard by restraining her at the portico. She tried her best to break away from our grasp, and at that point she appeared like an immeasurable source of energy. After a fierce struggle, we succeeded in holding her in check. The gust of wind shook the ancestral house driving Veronica into tantrums, the star lights and festoons kept oscillating. Like a ballet, the shadows also responded to the oscillations through subtle movements, the bells dangling on the fir tree chimed softly. Veronica stood disoriented, staring into the darkness. Even then, she expected something miraculous. Finally, she uttered in a quivering voice, 'My daughter was here . . . I evidently felt her presence.'

A feeling akin to an electric shock passed through my body, germinating the seeds of fear in the heart. We guided Veronica back to the room and I sat beside her, holding her hand. Her pounding pulse transmitted spasms of rhythm through my palm. We were all aghast at the strange happenings. The nervous uneasiness displayed by the horses, the gust of wind which opened the door and then blew out the candles, all contributed to the depth of the enigma. My mind regained calm, and I tried to comfort Veronica by quoting verses from the scriptures, and massaged her hands gently. Her husband and son stood nervously as silent witnesses to my efforts.

We were overwhelmed by an eerie silence slowly, and on account of acute uneasiness I made an attempt in vain to start a conversation. Fortunately, Veronica herself took the initiative to peel off the uneasy blanket of silence with a tale that transported us back to three decades.

The ancestral home of Tresa was anxious yet hopeful on a moonlit night. Her dad paced up and down anxiously, and the beautiful household was heading towards the pleasant experience of a birth. At frequent intervals, members of the household cast glances towards the closed door of the bedroom which was converted to a makeshift labour room. The dull pain which commenced at six in the evening progressed and intensified with the passage of time. After a prolonged labour of six hours, exactly at midnight, the walls of the ancestral home echoed with the wail of a newborn. With intense relief, they all thanked the Almighty. After handing over the child wrapped in a cotton sheet to the father, the doctor returned. After a while, Veronica accepted the child from him as if receiving a precious gift and that was the origin of a series of divine events in the life of Veronica, which spanned seventeen years.

'When I held her close to my chest, the baby wriggled and it sent waves of electricity through my body,' said Veronica. Her emotions strengthened every moment.

That night she could not part the child from her bosom. Holding the baby tight to her chest, she stood near the window which commanded a panoramic view of the landscape. The moon shone brightly casting silver rays all over the valley, the flora swayed gently in light breeze and as never before the sky was studded with countless stars. The twinkling stars appeared to have an element of life, and even nature appeared dressed for the occasion to receive the divine child.

That night, Veronica started experiencing peace and joy beyond words, she felt her heart easing of pain with the newborn at her bosom, and the lamp lighted that night stayed shining for the next seventeen years. Like a 'flame on the pedestal' that radiance remained as a blessing for thousands of people. The recollections of Veronica went on and on and on. I bade goodbye reluctantly at late night. Just before stepping out of the portico, she held my hand firmly and spoke softly in my ears.

'Do you know who blew the candles out . . . it was my daughter . . . she had been here.'

13

The highest peak in the heights had always fascinated me. It was in the grassland at the foot of the peak where Tresa had met her end. Reports of posthumous sightings of her in the vicinity of the peak heightened my curiosity. I wanted to set foot on the summit to mediate on the scriptures in the untrammelled calm of isolation.

Exactly twenty days before Christmas, in the company of Yohannan, I proceeded to the summit. The sharpness of the winter was relatively blunt on that day, as if by divine intervention. We waded through the forest and the rumbling of the waterfall intensified at every step. Through the thick canopy of leaves the sunbeams percolated with difficulty; we negotiated the difficult terrain of the forests like acrobats walking on a tightrope and arrived near the swift-flowing stream which appeared like a silver sash that day. The torrent dives to a depth of more than a hundred metres at a point that was nearly half a kilometre downstream of where we stood. We headed for the waterfall moving downstream parallel to the raging current.

The waterfall appeared like the ooze of liquefied silver. In the backdrop of its powerful rumbling, the drops scattered by the wind painted the seven colours in the air and inspired in us the feeling of being at the gates of heaven.

I spotted two human forms, not far from where the waterfall slams onto the land. It was none other than the 'Queen of Prostitutes' and her son. She was slamming the laundry onto a rock, and her son was playing not far away. The shawl that had blown away from me a few days back covered the child. They were no longer merely half alive—that morning I found them beaming with energy and vigour. My heart filled with immense joy since my answers to the vicar's question had turned meaningful, and it was certain that it was the Almighty Himself who received warmth and comfort through the shawl. I realized that I was on the right track in pursuit of God.

Yohannan knocked me up from these deep thoughts. He was pointing downwards and forced me to look in that direction. 'The Queen of Prostitutes' was looking at us, pressing the laundry to her bosom, and I could not gauge the expression in her eyes because of the distance. Yohannan sprang up and started walking, uttering curses at her. I followed him casting backward glances at regular intervals, and found her eyes focused on us. We moved upstream and kept on walking along the banks of the stream.

I enquired about the logic behind doing the laundry in the morning.

'Don't you know . . . to stay away from the sight of others,' Yohannan responded furiously.

Leaving the banks of the stream, we negotiated the steep ascent. Yohannan knew the intricate capillaries of the forest tracks like the back of his hand. Swinging on the jungle vines and treading on the stones, we came out of the dense forest.

Right in front of our eyes stretched the extensive grasslands, and the peak towering over the vastness stood tall. We waded through the thick mass of grass. It was somewhere here that Tresa had met her end. I cast my glance in different directions. Like concealing an unforgivable sin, the glass blades stood tall, and on account of overwhelming emotions my heart grew heavy.

There was a light breeze and the grass murmured. Thick curls of smoke were issuing from the forest bordering the grassland.

'That is the tribal colony,' said Yohannan pointing at thin curls of smoke.

He gave a clear and detailed account of the aborigine settlements. These inhabitants of the heights hunt in dense forests, their cattle thrive in the grasslands, and using the traditional method of agriculture they mine 'gold' in the fertile lands where the forests meet the grasslands. Yohannan as a missionary frequents these colonies. Their traditional armoury consists of bow and arrow, and even the guns of the British who came to the heights struggled hard at first to match their archery skills.

According to the vicar it was the aborigines who spotted the body of Tresa, they are the ones who guarded the body and helped bring her to the church. I prayed for these souls who are in spirit as pure as the Lily of the Valley.

Traversing the grassland we finally reached the foot of the highest peak which stood elegantly crowned with vapour like the king of the ranges. The pieces of rocks on the slopes appeared like the rungs of a ladder, and to scale the peak to set foot on the summit one had to tread on those. On the acclivity towards the summit there were woods, streams and waterfalls, and it turned out to be a severe battle to climb up. I raised my eyes to the zenith and sensing the insurmountable nature of the summit, my heart fluttered in fear.

We devoted a short span of time for rest and then braced ourselves for the toughest part of the journey. After praying fervently for a few minutes for the protection of the Almighty, taking a deep breath we proceeded towards the peak.

Our ascent began, the heart throbbed like a drum and the leg muscles stretched like a string. On account of the physical exertions, at times we even struggled to breathe. The energy triggered by the prayer acted as a catalyst on the journey, and the slippery rocks, chill and the fickle mist tried in vain to dampen our enthusiasm. The chill intensified with altitude and the nature of flora kept changing with the ascent. We were getting elevated to a new world, and in the process the uneasy whistling of the wind almost pierced the ear drum. We rested at regular intervals, throwing glances into the horizon and enjoying the sight of massive fort-like ranges of the Western Ghats with valleys appearing like smudged green.

The vegetation kept thinning out with altitude; what remained before the summit was grassland and we moved through the knee-deep grass.

The trees leaning out from the steep slopes appeared human, as if about to throw themselves into the abyss. I tried in vain to get a sight of the summit, and it looked like a never-ending climb. Slowly the grasslands gave way to slippery slopes and we continued with utmost care. Any slight distraction or a fraction of aberration would result in a fatal plunge thousands of feet down. Suddenly, we got enveloped by a thick pall of mist which reduced visibility to almost nil, and we were scared to pause on the steep slope even for a second. With sincere prayers, we groped and climbed, and suddenly in a sudden gust of wind the blanket of the mist detached itself from the peak. The azure of the sky appeared to our sight and announced the successful conclusion of a difficult mission. Yohannan reached the summit first and with the help of his extended hand I set my foot upon the peak. For a few minutes we sat on the summit panting like dogs.

We stood up after a short rest and started enjoying the sights that were beyond words. It gave us the feeling of standing on top of the world with the ranges kneeling down obsequiously. The cloud flakes drifted in the air, the valley appeared flattened out like a green carpet and it turned out to be an experience akin to heaven. Exactly at the middle of the summit stood a boulder and a dwarf tree. We sat at the bottom of the tree drawing the shawl over the body. Intoxicated by the natural beauty, I yearned for permanence in that tiny version of paradise. I came under the grip of a superiority complex and was overwhelmed by a sense of authority. For a moment I felt the authority of the world vested in me, and the feeling of being bestowed with elegance, titles, positions and glory came creeping into my heart.

Yohannan opened his rucksack, took the Bible and unfolded it; shortly an interesting passage flowed on to the summit through his voice.

The Christ ascends to the top of a mountain with his disciples. At the summit of the mountain, he transforms into an apparition which as bright as thousands of stars. The disciples see Christ in conversation with the Prophets Elijah and Moses upon his death on the cross.

On witnessing the Christ in all his heavenly splendour, the hearts of the disciples get intoxicated and they say:

'Master, let us remain here. We will pitch three tents . . . one for you, one for Moses and one for Elijah.'

Christ descends from the mountain, heedless of the disciples, to carry out the most difficult mission of death on the cross. At the foot of the mountain, the multitudes envelope them like a raging current and the presence of Christ delivers them from pains and ailments.

Yohannan concluded the rendition of the gospel and my heart staggered at the verses. I felt each and every word in the gospel, standing erect, pointing fingers at me, and commanding me to return to the valley of hardships, to associate myself with the souls who were poor, naked, sorrowful and ill.

I remained silent for a few minutes, engraving the message of the gospel on my mind and heart, deeply. Suddenly Yohannan pointed his fingers at the horizon; my eyes followed, and clearly saw another peak as towering as this, afar. In spite of the bright sunshine it had a horrifying dark tint.

'That is the infamous dark mountain,' said Yohannan.

'What makes it infamous?' I threw the question at Yohannan.

'It is blanketed with very dense forests . . . that is where the most notorious witchdoctor who scares the heights to the core lives.'

Through the clutter of indigenous stories and traditions, right from childhood I was aware of the witchdoctor who supposedly lived in the hostile slopes of the dark mountain.

'It is not possible to see this mountain from the church complex.' added Yohannan.

'According to the aborigines, the practice of human sacrifice is still very much alive in the Dark Mountain. We should go there one day to drive that evil man out of the heights . . . but it calls for preparations like intense fasting prayer and more spiritual growth.'

The clouds enveloped the Dark Mountain and its ugly elevation sent shudders through my heart. The Dark Mountain appeared like an evil castle, amassing and housing the forces of darkness to be unleashed at an unexpected hour. My mind grew uneasy and I clearly felt the inevitability of a collision with the dweller of the Dark Mountain sooner or later.

Through fervent prayers, I calmed myself down. When the sun started slanting westwards, we descended the mountain with renewed missions and revised goals.

14

With heightened curiosity about the Dark Mountain, I returned to the vicarage and the prolonged influence of the evil mountain prompted me to pace to and fro in the vicarage. After dinner, I retired to the bedroom faintly illuminated by the lantern and stood near the window casting glances towards the landscape.

The heights shone in the bright moonlight and the moon appeared hanging over the ranges. An irresistible temptation to enjoy the aromatic air, in the moonlight, near the tomb of Tresa surfaced in my heart. I requested Esteppan for his company; suddenly the expression of fear rushed onto his face but he acceded to my request with profound reluctance.

Outside, the silvery landscape greeted us and the ranges looked like walls plated with silver. We walked parallel to the church complex and reached the entrance of the cemetery. Esteppan pushed the huge gate slightly and made a little gap for us just to squeeze ourselves in. Before us appeared the extensive ground with hundreds of tombs and headstones. The creeper in full bloom, which obscured the tomb of Tresa, looked like a bright speck from afar.

Esteppan hesitated and wanted to go back. Heedless of his hesitation, I moved forward. He was forced to follow me and we tread through the inmost parts of the cemetery with careful steps. In the gentle breeze, the blades of grass twisted and turned, hissing like snakes, and we waded through the intricate maze of tombstones, struggling to maintain balance. With every step, the aroma of the divine flowers intensified.

We sat near the tomb. Flakes of clouds drifted above and thousands of stars twinkled in the sky. The moon was in its full elegance. I was overwhelmed, not by the natural eerie feeling of the cemetery, but by the enticing beauty of the moonlit night. Esteppan was in an entirely different mood which made his voice feeble and shaking.

I grabbed the palm of Esteppan and prayed. His fear eased considerably. After the prayer, we sat in silence for a few moments enjoying the gentle strokes of nature who with a paintbrush coated the scene with moonlight.

'Esteppan, have you ever heard of the Dark Mountain?'

Esteppan instantly responded to my question with a violent shudder.

Esteppan gave me a detailed account of the Dark Mountain. In the heights, the Dark Mountain stands second in terms of elevation. The valley and the foot of the mountain are covered with dense forest. Nobody from the civilized world would like to set foot on the Dark Mountain. The environs of the mountain are infested with venomous snakes, reptiles and members of the cat family. That is where the most notorious witch doctor lives. His sole communication with the world is through the aborigines who worship evil. According to many early inhabitants, even the water spouted by the springs and flowing through the tiny capillaries of streams in the Dark Mountain are black in colour. The slopes are honeycombed with countless caves. In the view of some aborigines the mysterious, remotest corners of the mountain witness even human sacrifices.

On hearing this, I was numb in disbelief. Even at first sight, the threat posed by the Dark Mountain was quite clear, and its enigmatic appearance triggered ripples of fear in me. I tried to refocus my attention on the cool, comforting moonlight.

The walls of the church echoed the notes of celestial music and the congregation got enveloped in a translucence of smoke laden with incense. Tempted by the moonlight, I stepped out of the church. The entire landscape remained drenched in the lunar radiance and the winking stars in the sky appeared no longer inanimate. Like a soul hypnotized by nature, I crossed the extensive lawn at the front yard of the church. I felt disoriented and kept on moving as if under the influence of a strange force. Because of the moonlight the tip of the grass blades shone like points on needles. Like a well-orchestrated ballet, the flora swayed in the breeze. With soft steps I crossed the lawn and descended to the depths of the forests. The moonlight filtering through the canopy of trees looked like threads of silver piercing the forest bed. Unusually, that night, the forest was devoid of the chirping of crickets. It felt like a wonderland.

Instantly, the shine of the moon waned. Suddenly the forest was flooded with the shrill cry of crickets which pierced my ear. The sudden change in the mood of nature was unbearable for me. My heart fluttered wildly, and I screamed. I could not move an inch because of the thick blanket of darkness that engulfed the surroundings unexpectedly. The uneasy cries of an evil bird sent harpoons through my heart.

In the depth of darkness, someone touched me. Shuddering and shivering, I stood with a racing heart. The thick blanket of clouds which obscured the moon melted away and the radiance of the moon resurfaced gradually. In utmost fear, I turned around slowly to catch a glimpse of the object which had come into contact with me.

The beautiful golden hair drifting in the air . . . the well sculpted, perfectly symmetrical countenance . . . like a thread for a drowning soul—in a flash I grabbed the hand of Tresa, and the fears vanished in an instant. She held me close instilling a tremendous sense of security into my heart. Like an angel, she guided me back. We reached the church crossing the extensive front yard drenched in silver.

Near the entrance of the church we stood face to face, in the light breeze, her golden hair was cascading down and her face shone with the radiance of celestial bodies. In her smile my worries were effaced completely. The divine grace which shone on her left a permanent mark on my mind. She led me back to the church, and both of us plunged into the divine waves of worship.

Esteppan knocked me up from the recollection of an incident that took place sixteen years ago on a Christmas night.

'Let us go back please,' pleaded Esteppan. He was evidently under the grip of fear.

'Esteppan . . . Tresa has been reportedly seen by many after death. Is there any truth in this?' I launched the most perplexing question. Esteppan responded with a shudder, and fear became apparent on his face.

'Fear not . . . I am here.' I gave him my reassurances.

Suddenly the moonlight weakened considerably, covering the entire cemetery with the pall of darkness. With a beating heart, I raised my eyes to the skies, and the moon re-emerged from a thick, large cloud.

'Let us go. . . . '

This time Esteppan's voice sounded more pathetic. I tried to strengthen him, concealing my own apprehensions about the sudden variation in the moonlight. Esteppan reluctantly gave up his insistence.

'Only a few people have witnessed this. Recently there was a reported sighting near the cemetery. Fleeing in fear, the man fell down and suffered injuries . . . remained feverish for a week.' Esteppan announced in a fluttering voice, and he remained like an overstretched string, with the possibility of snapping anytime.

Suddenly the moonlight faded again. With heightened fear, again we raised our eyes to the skies. Another cloud of considerable radius was concealing the moon. From the wilderness came the wailing and howling of wild dogs and wolves. I unknowingly raised myself from the seating position and cast glances coated with fear.

'Let us go. . . . '

This time Esteppan nearly wept. All of a sudden the distant forest became obscured by a whirling fog which was stretching itself, and I sagaciously judged this phenomenon as the forerunner of disaster. The howling of wolves was on the ascent and dogs in the heights responded to the wailing. We both darted towards the entrance of the cemetery and struggled to find our way in the waning light. In the desperate rush for safety, we unknowingly tread on the tombstones. Every second, the howling kept on scaling new heights and like fire tainted with moisture, the moonlight almost vanished. I cursed myself for ignoring the warnings of Esteppan and squeezed out through the narrow gap between the wall and the slightly opened gate.

The moonlight was almost turned off, the entire landscape got enveloped in the thickness of the mist and we dashed towards the vicarage. The presence of the evil power close on our heels was palpable, and the moment we ran past the church complex the moon-light got extinguished fully. Then the thick eddy of mist encircled us, the howling of the wild almost reached its zenith. In the poor visibility we faltered, fumbled, and scraped against the walls and finally reached the security of the vicarage. Heaving a sigh of relief I returned to the bedroom which was lit by a lantern, and the faint gleam of the flame appeared like bright sunshine for me.

The thickness of the mist pushed firmly against the glass window as if determined to shatter it. Under the loud howling of the wild the vicarage trembled. My anxiety and fear kept spiralling upwards. It was evident that some kind of unearthly power was at large in the heights at night. This unpleasant experience lasted for half an hour and gradually died down. The moonlight unshackled itself from the grip of clouds drenching the heights again in silver, and on that night I was able to sleep only after fervent prayers.

15

Augustine lived in a two-storey house donated by the parents of Tresa. The elevated surface on which the house rested necessitated a climb of nearly fifty steps and at the exact middle of the extensive front yard stood a dwarf tree coiled with a creeper called the 'golden trumpet'. The flowers that bloomed on the creeper were trumpet-shaped, golden in colour and on account of the profusion of flowers on the creeper the dwarf tree appeared like a pillar of fire in the extensive green.

Augustine and Veronica received us with warmth and overflowing affection. We sat on the veranda enjoying the lukewarm beams of the sun and immersed ourselves in a deep conversation. Augustine and Veronica recalled my deeds and misdeeds as a child fifteen years back, and we were all ears to their narratives, cracked jokes and enjoyed ourselves immensely. The tea provided by the daughter-in-law of Veronica turned out to be energizing and appealing to the palate.

Then came a slight pause in the conversation, and I turned my attention to nature. It was a clear day; the veranda commanded a clear view of the majestic ranges, the sun was on its journey to the west, and we were all overwhelmed by the enthusiasm inspired by the light chill carried by the breeze. Suddenly, Yohannan diverted the conversation to Tresa and enquired about the cause behind her death. Immediately Augustine's face fell, Veronica became tearful, their body language underwent a sea change with the shoulders of Augustin drooping and Veronica hung her head in grief. Both of them came under the vice-like grip of sorrow.

Then Augustine responded in a broken voice talked about the death of Tresa. Since the brightness of the sun appeared fading gradually, I looked towards the sky and found the sun emerging from a dark drifting cloud, the shadow of which went past through the extensive lawn of the front yard. The sudden emergence of the cloud in the clear sky astonished me to the core, and despite apparent uneasiness, I refocused on the narrative of Augustine. A few minutes later, again the sun got eclipsed considerably, and I gazed towards the skies.

Like the invasion of a frenzied dark army, the clouds conquered every nook and corner of the sky and obscured the sun with a thick canopy. The narrative of Augustine progressed, and Yohannan listened to him attentively, then came the lashing of a strong wind swaying the treetops violently, and the wooden window frames in the house slammed under its force. The dwarf tree laden with golden flowers fluttered like a flame in the wind.

The rumbling of horizons unsettled my mind, the streaks of lightning twisted and turned over the peaks. Within moments, the entire expanse of the sky turned dark, and nature looked sorrowful.

Augustine told his tale, and Yohannan remained at the peak of excitement which made me doubtful whether his body was in contact with the chair or not. Augustine's narration reached the summit. Suddenly the wind ceased and nature stood still. In a quivering voice, Augustine divulged the cause of Tresa's death.

A lightning whizzed past dazzling us for a few minutes, and close on its heels came an earth-shattering thunder. Like an arrow, the words uttered by Augustine struck me and pierced my heart. In the paroxysm of agony I wriggled and cried, and under its impact even the fury of nature appeared next to nothing.

Like a ferocious animal broken free from a chain, the wind lashed, the trees swayed, and countless twigs and dry leaves, rained onto the Veranda.

Thick raindrops hurtled down and slammed onto the earth. With a heart-shattering scream Veronica ran out, embraced the swaying dwarf tree, slammed her head on that and cried. Like blood-stained tears, nature rained golden flowers on her.

I cried uncontrollably, Yohannan struggled immensely to hold his tears back and Augustine sat depressed with restrained sobs. Under the impact of the shock, we remained for a few moments completely oblivious of Veronica who was receiving the battering of nature. The cries of nature went on and on and on. On regaining his presence of mind, Yohannan ran out and embraced Veronica who remained fully drenched with golden flowers. With the care of an affectionate son, he brought her back to the veranda.

Gradually the lamentations of nature died down, the noise of streaming raindrops from the roof overwhelmed the surroundings, and like solidified grief the sky remained fully overcast.

My mind remained fully numb; even without saying adieu to the host, I left the house with swaying steps. I felt fully drained, devoid of energy from every cell, and my body shuddered and shivered under intense grief. My mind felt shattered into thousands of fragments. Yohannan supported my body that was fully drained of energy and enthusiasm, and with his help I waded to the vicarage with unsteady steps.

16

On reaching the vicarage I took refuge in the bedroom without consuming even a drop of water or a crumb of food, and struggled on account of an uneasy heaviness in the chest. Every cell in my body had been throbbing with energy since my arrival at the heights. Each and every organ in my body had been the reservoir of strength. The pulsating energy made me capable of twisting even iron bars in pursuit of missions, but that immeasurable quantum of strength now appeared completely drained on learning the cause of Tresa's death.

I threw myself onto the bed with a shattered heart and covered my face in the blanket. On those occasions when the heaviness of the chest reached unbearable levels, I got up and paced up and down like an insane. Darkness kept on unfolding over the heights gradually, and the valleys came under the grip of thick mist. Like the teardrops of an angel a drizzle started and I felt nature associating itself with the grief in my mind.

Contrary to the routine, I failed to light the lantern in the evening and wished to perish in the dark hands of darkness. Sometime in the evening Esteppan came and breathed the radiance of life into the lantern. I heard the evening prayers of the vicar while plunging into the abyss of desperation, and turned down the invitation of Esteppan for dinner. I remained fully aware of the advancement of the hours. At night, I made up my mind to fasten onto the scriptures which had been of immense value in crises in the past.

In the light of the lantern, I unfolded the scriptures. Unlike the past I failed to experience the electrifying thrill which used to originate from the Bible. I was not able to experience the throbbing of the heart in heavenly bliss. The letters and verses appeared as mere impressions of a printing machine, and that night, the scriptures turned out to be a mere inanimate collection of records bound in leather.

Again overwhelmed by uneasiness, I paced up and down the room. The other inhabitants of the vicarage were in sound sleep. My heart rate accelerated by leaps and bounds, and even in the dim light I noticed the changes in the colour of my palm, which had turned deep red. On closer observation, the wriggle of the vein below the palm became apparent, and it kept on twisting and turning with every pulsation. With a shudder, I came to grips with the fact that the blood pressure within my body was scaling alarming levels due to heightened stress. I started sweating profusely in spite of the nip in the air and feared the possibility of an imminent cardiac arrest.

After a while, my mind became attuned to the variation in the heartbeat. In the span of that interim relief, I took the scriptures and proceeded to the room of the vicar with unsteady steps. Through the darkness of the corridor I inched forward to his room.

I stood before the room of the vicar for an instant, then slowly pushed the door which opened with a screech and stepped into the room with a shivering body and weary mind. The vicar was awake in the faintly lit room, and he looked obviously disturbed at the changes which had taken possession of me. The vicar rose, sat on the bed and then looked at me in bewilderment.

I knelt with an aching heart, placed the scriptures and rosary before him, touched his feet, apologized and announced my decision to renounce the path of spirituality. I endured the squeezing pain in my heart and the tears which flowed profusely through my cheeks drenched the feet of the vicar. The vicar sat with stooping shoulders, hanging his head in distress. In that posture, the stoop on his back appeared aggravated to a great extent. He remained silent for a few seconds.

'Dear Child.'

I responded favourably to the voice of the vicar that sounded like the broken strings of a lute.

'I am well aware of the circumstances which drove you madly to this decision. Fifteen years back, I was also on the verge of renouncing the path of the Almighty. But I prayed a lot and prayer has power. The divine truth which dawned on me those days still gives me the strength to move along the path of the divine in spite of ill health and advanced age.'

While speaking, he ran his fingers through my hair.

'I was akin to the disciples who were scattered from the garden of Gethsemane. In fear they lurked in a room devoid of courage to step out even for an instant. They cursed themselves . . . they were scared even of the light.'

Suddenly the body language of the vicar underwent a noticeable transition. He held his head high . . . the stooping shoulders got straight . . . he pointed his finger afar and said, 'After a few days the disciples who were fear-stricken came to the exact centre of Jerusalem. They were no longer afraid. Their eyes sparkled with hope and they were beaming with confidence, shining like celestial bodies . . . they proclaimed the resurrection of Jesus.'

The vicar placed his hands on my shoulders and said, 'Please pray without cease . . . the treasure trove of divine truths would be unlocked before you . . . come and meet me after a fortnight. If you still maintain your views, then I will not discourage you from abandoning the path of spirituality.'

I turned back to leave. Suddenly the vicar grabbed my hand and said with a sob, 'I will pray for you around the clock.'

I detached his hand from mine mercilessly and walked back, severing the link with spirituality, once for all. Only at the break of dawn was I able to find some sleep.

17

The next day I woke up with a weary mind and found the heights fully blanketed in mist. The presence of fog and the absence of sunshine pushed me into the abyss of gloom.

After a long gap of many years, the deep-rooted routine of morning prayer and meditation over scriptures got disrupted. I refused breakfast and on account of the growing heaviness in the chest paced up and down through the room like a skunk.

Contrary to the normal, the mist lasted till the afternoon. Under the compulsion of Esteppan and Devassy I had lunch as a mere formality. The veil of the mist started thinning out in the afternoon and it started drizzling. This time, under the overcast sky, the greenery of the landscape did not appear amplified. Instead, the land looked colourless and monotonous and the canopy of tea gardens seemed like an old worn-out carpet. I had been in possession of throbbing confidence and sturdy determination till yesterday; hope and optimism guided me till now. Above all, I strongly believed in the influence and guidance of the Almighty in my words and deeds. But that moment, the motivator, the spirituality, existed like a cage of bones, fully stripped of flesh and marrow.

I kept on rambling about till the evening, and in spite of suffering muscle cramps, I felt scared to pause even for a second. My heavy heart endured the pain of getting squashed by the iron fists of disaster, and eventually the process of breathing also grew difficult.

The overcast sky guided the darkness to the heights earlier than usual. Despite my distressed mind, I noticed the darkness gaining predominance in the room and enveloping the landscape. Devassy took over the responsibility of lighting the lantern, and that evening the flame of the lamp struggled considerably to push the darkness out.

I ate dinner reluctantly and mechanically, and after returning to the bedroom again unthinkingly paced up and down. It had been nearly twenty-four hours after severing the umbilical cord with the scriptures. On account of a hair-splitting headache, I was finally forced to recline in bed.

Something knocked me up from the short nap. The flame of the lantern flickered unusually as if the flickering were triggered by something else, and I looked at the shivering flame in awe. At frequent intervals of micro seconds, it shuddered and shivered. I raised my right arm which was resting on the table which had the lantern. In an instant, the fluttering stopped and the flame started glowing steadily. I was shocked at the realization that the fluttering of the flame had been caused by the vibrations of my racing pulse rate, and feared my capillaries were on the verge of rupturing.

At night, an excruciating pain in the head knocked me up; suspecting the onset of a stroke, I sprang up like lightning and found myself drenched in sweat, and the rhythm of my heart sounded like a drum which prompted me to pace to and fro again through the room. The prolonged stress of nearly forty-eight hours made me totally disoriented, and on account of the weariness I frequently edged and elbowed the furniture while moving.

In the late hours, I slept for a while. While plummeting and drifting through the world of slumber, I clearly made out the presence of the vicar in my room, his gentle touch on my forehead and prayers for my welfare. His visits provided me with temporary relief.

Next morning I woke up with heightened anxiety and felt a severe pain in the left arm and shoulders. On account of the alarming heart rate, seeds of fear started sprouting in my mind. To ease the mounting pressure, I started moving again through the room, and struggled for a firm footing as I was feeling light headed. At regular intervals I experienced pain in my shoulder and left arm which stepped up my anxiety, I even interpreted these as the symptoms of a cardiac problem.

Suddenly my body sweated profusely and made me feel alarmed; in an attempt to reach the vicar I stepped out of the room, hobbling. Much to my relief, Esteppan rushed towards me and gave support, and he called in the medical team. After a detailed examination, they came to the conclusion that the functioning of my heart was satisfactory. They diagnosed tachycardia and high blood pressure. The doctors confirmed the health of my heart and strongly recommended the maintenance of composure; then they left having labelled the symptoms as sheer panic attack.

The medical opinion which reaffirmed the health of my heart gave me some relief. Till then I had never been worried or bothered about my health, and with the support of the scriptures I used to defuse turbulence and crises, unfazed. But on that occasion, I felt like a warrior devoid of weapons.

On the next day, on hearing my difficulties, Yohannan called in with a few evangelists. They did their best to bolster my faith through prayers and the rendition of scriptures. Neither my body nor my mind responded to the efforts of the evangelists favourably, and my mind mercilessly warded off the waves of prayers and the rendition of scriptures. The unpleasant throbbing of the heart continued uninterrupted.

Finally Yohannan and the evangelists left the room, crestfallen. The dark tint of disappointment on the face of Yohannan came to my notice, even in that awkward situation. The vicar continued his visits to my room at regular intervals. It was quite evident that the vicar was on another spell of intense fasting prayer. At night even in slumber I could clearly make out the gentle touch of the vicar immersed in affection. His prayers and tears were powerful enough to melt my hardened heart. But like the Pharaoh of Egypt referred in the Book of Exodus, I resisted all these efforts by hardening my mind and heart on purpose.

Since my faith remained in absolute shambles, I kept on resisting. I profoundly regretted the moment of embarking on the journey along the path of spirituality, a sense of meaninglessness took deep root in my mind. The following days my condition deteriorated considerably, and the situation was going from bad to worse. In spite of the hectic schedule of Advent, the vicar went ahead with the series of severe fasting prayers. I scoffed at his meditations in my mind as mere futile exercises.

I was on the verge of mental disintegration; occasionally a sense of getting close to death dawned on me. The fear of an impending cardiac arrest kept me on tenterhooks, and even the clear diagnosis of the doctors failed to ease the fear. I feared my days were numbered, and at night I was knocked up many times by a lashing sensation caused by the soaring blood pressure. At times, like a disoriented person I tried to run out of the vicarage screaming at the top of my voice. It called for the collective efforts of Devassy and Esteppan to keep me under restraint.

On the following days I came under the grip of panic attacks at regular intervals, and many times shuddered under the mirage of strokes and cardiac arrests. At the request of the vicar, an extremely skilled medical team rushed to the vicarage, and they reiterated the diagnosis of 'panic attacks'. In the intervals of freedom from the panic attacks, I preferred to remain in my room giving utterances to curses, and kept on pacing up and down to keep the mental agony in check.

I turned a blind eye, on purpose, to the prayers of the vicar for me and viewed with intense scorn the efforts of the vicar to pray for my total recovery. Under the intensity of anger and disappointment, I yearned to throw myself into the abyss of all kinds of evil and vices. Once again I was drifting towards the fearful black hole. I brushed aside the request from the vicar to partake in the Holy Communion on Sunday.

Just ten days before Christmas, I came under the grip of a strong fever with a constant cough and breathing difficulties. The medical team concluded that the difficulties were triggered by a severe infection in the chest. Esteppan and Davessy administered the medicines to me forcibly, and I felt the icy hands of death. On account of high fever my body fluttered like the tense string of a bow, and the smooth expansion and contraction of the lungs remained hampered as if laden with weight. Even at the height of the crisis, I refused to touch the scriptures; in other words I was poles apart from the Almighty.

Esteppan forced me to inhale steam issuing from the boiling water saturated with herbs of high medicinal value. In spite of the sincere efforts on the part of Esteppan I pushed myself desperately into the abyss of the black hole. So intense was my desperation and so my hope deteriorated.

On the teeth-chattering night of December 23rd, like a wilted balsam stem, I remained stretched on the bed with high fever. The cinders burning in the fireplace appeared ineffective against the darkness, and the blanket which wrapped my body failed to make the chill less intense. The intensity of the fever could not mitigate the burning anger and frustration in my mind.

While drifting into a light slumber, a strange light that intensified every moment came to my attention. I clearly saw the flames of candles and gradually the image of an altar appeared in my vision.

The golden hair cascading in the breeze . . . the apparition of the angel stood at the altar lighting a long row of candles. The intensifying light not only threw the altar into sharp relief but also the bas-reliefs on the dome. With soft steps, with a curiosity galloping ahead every second, I came close to her. Without turning her face she extended her arm backwards, towards me. I grabbed her hand and slowly she started drifting in the air, and like a ribbon attached to the finger of the angel I also ascended. Then appeared before us in the twilight the vague outline of the ranges and tall trees, and as if powered by a divine invisible energy we drifted through the canopy of treetops. I clearly heard the notes of celestial music and the waves of the angelic music followed us. Suddenly a faint gleam appeared afar like a speck. It kept on growing every second, and we drifted towards the unfolding radiance. Piercing the thick screen of jungle vines we touched down near the radiance.

We found ourselves in a dilapidated, abandoned temple in the interiors of the thick forests, from the pillars of which protruded the once beautiful sculptures carved in stone. In the radiance of a strange light, the temple was well illuminated. I was shocked after noticing that not even an iota of flame was present there and was overjoyed at the realization that the walls of the temple were turned radiant by the flames lighted on the altar miles away. I stood in the flooding light, in utter amazement, and then turned my face to catch a glimpse of the cherub who had carried me there.

18

I rose from slumber and remained seated for a few minutes, totally disoriented. The faint gleam of a lantern greeted me, and what I had experienced a few moments back as a deluge of illumination was no longer in existence. I experienced the weariness of an intergalactic journey spanning many light years, and my body was profusely drenched in sweat.

Gradually the heart rate started gaining normalcy, the fever and breathlessness eased considerably and the lungs appeared recouping by casting off all the unwarranted heaviness.

I was not able to write off the experience as mere delusion or illusion, and somewhere in the deep dark abyss of hopelessness appeared a speck of light. In the scriptures, there are clear references about the dreams which turned out to be meaningful. Like Joseph who interpreted the dreams of the Pharaoh of Egypt, I started to extricate the details of the experience akin to an illusion.

The altar and bas-relief which appeared in the dream seemed extremely familiar; although I could not get a glance of the face, it became well evident that the angelic apparition was none other than Tresa since the softness of the touch triggered celestial bliss in me. The dilapidated temple at the heart of the forest brought back the recollections of the visit I had paid to the place with Tresa in our childhood. Suddenly with great exaltation I realized that it was the flame lighted on the altar that had illuminated the abandoned temple located miles away. My heart raced, the message of the divine pierced into my heart like an arrow: 'expand the ken beyond the four walls of my religion', and the burning smoulders in my mind hissed and went out as if slammed by the rain of rose water.

I broke away from the gravitational pull of the black hole and started drifting towards the land of the living. All of a sudden, a craving for opening the scriptures and to imbibe the message of the divine dawned on me. On account of the interlude of peace after the gap of many days, I was able to find sound sleep.

I felt more energetic in the morning, and the only Achilles' heel was the lethargy inflicted by prolonged illness. The change in the manner of the vicar who visited me in the morning appeared very obvious. Till the day before, his face had been lifeless and tense, but that morning he was as radiant as a constellation. He appeared fully devoid of the stoop, and his eyes sparkled with joy. Overflowing with affection he gently touched my cheeks and once again I felt the current transmitted through his fingers, completely inundating all the cells in my body. I smiled at him, my joyful expression raised his spirits, and his face throbbed with happiness.

I responded positively to the request of the vicar to partake in the Christmas service and Holy Communion that night. The vicar decided to arrange for Yohannan to be present to provide an emotional support for me, then he left the room to plunge himself again into the hectic preparations for the Advent.

Throughout that day I slept peacefully, like a newborn, recouped, and then proceeded to the church accompanied by Yohannan. After an interval of nearly three weeks, I crossed the threshold of the vicarage. I clad myself in warm clothes. Since traces of the ailment remained with me, at times I lost my balance, and in those instances, Yohannan held me tight and supported me like a brother. His presence turned out to be a blessing on that night.

Illuminated with countless stars and lamps, the church complex shone like a nova. The turnout for the service was extremely large, and size of the congregation pushed us to the rear of the church which could accommodate very many people. The service commenced with the opening hymn; my body responded to the song, and the rendition of the scriptures filled my heart with exultation. My heart leapt at the references to the newborn in the manager who would be the blessing for all nations. The curtains parted and the altar appeared with the radiance of thousands of flames. The presence of two new vicars on the altar compensated for my absence fully. The incense containers oscillated in metallic rhythm, and the curls of smoke issued by the smouldering incense stood as a translucent barrier between the altar and the congregation.

My mind throbbed with energy inducing an irresistible desire to rush to the altar and partake in the service. Again I felt like proceeding through the designated pathway to the Lord and getting elevated to the higher altitudes of spirituality. At intervals, the dormant ailment surfaced in the form of severe cough and on those occasions Yohannan, patting my back, held me close. Once again I returned to the stage of an infant who is taking the first steps on the path of spirituality, Yohannan transformed into a guardian saddled with heavy responsibilities, and I remained fully engrossed in the divine beauty of the service.

At the beginning of the Holy Communion, Yohanaan guided me to the altar where I knelt to accept the sacraments. The melodious rendition of the choir echoed from the walls of the church. In the radiance of candles and lamps the altar seemed coated with gold, the curls of fumes carrying the aroma of incense swirled in the church, and in the deluge of radiance, I encountered the feeling of levitating into another world. I raised my face at the sharp, crisp, short metallic sound of a steel spoon scraping against the inner walls of the chalice. Right before me stood the vicar who was in a glittering cassock; he placed the sacraments on my tongue and the sweet ripples of the wine transmitted all over my body. I returned to the seat at the rear more energetically without the support of Yohannan.

Yohannan proceeded back to the faith home after ensuring my comfort and welfare. Hundreds in the congregation stood lined up for receiving the sacraments, and the prolongation of service for one more hour appeared certain.

I cast glances through the arched window of the church, through which it was possible to get a clear view of the cemetery from the spot where I sat. On casting my glance in that direction, I sprang up involuntarily. I could not even believe my eyes. With insatiable curiosity and suppressed fear I stepped out of the church into the ground silvered by nature. Thousands of stars shone in the sky totally devoid of clouds. The forests, ranges and even the blades of grass stood bathed in silver leaving nature spellbound.

A strange phenomenon was taking shape in the cemetery and like a fog it snaked out through the bars of the iron gate. At the entrance, it started assuming human form and under the influence of a sudden breeze it turned, twisted, and straightened. The treetops and the grass moved, and my heart started racing. I restrained my fear and tried to get close to the phenomenon; it kept on drifting in the air, and appeared more human after the lapse of every second. Curious, I tailed the phenomenon, totally unaware of the surroundings.

The beauty of nature reached the pinnacle with the amplification of the moonlight; in the silvery radiance, every flora seemed to be bracing up for divine festivities. The gentle breeze carried the aroma of the divine flowers to every nook and corner in the vicinity of the church, and the divinity of that was capable of alleviating sorrow and gloom no matter how severe they were.

I kept on tailing the phenomenon and the gap between us shortened at every step. At close range, it started appearing like a woman. As if perfectly synchronized with the movements of the flora, the phenomenon swirled and turned. The star-studded sky also contributed to this beautiful setting by winking their eyes. The force of the winds reached its zenith, and the radiance of the moon reached incredible levels. Like a mad damsel, the treetops moved in the intensifying wind. I reached within an arm's length of the phenomenon; the long hair drifting in the wind seemed to have a golden tint and it coiled gently on my fingers. Suddenly the wind ceased, the radiance of the moon returned to normal. In the absence of the wind the wildly swaying treetops ceased and came to a standstill.

Right before me, the phenomenon melted into thin air and vanished. In an instant, the entire area came under the grip of a thick fog which melted away almost instantaneously. From the vanished mist emerged a group of people who were the committee members of the church. They requested me to return to the church immediately. They also added that some strange nocturnal forces are loitering in the heights and they were moving as a group in an attempt to decrypt the phenomenon. Affectionately, they reminded me of the dangers of moving about alone at night. I turned back and found the well-lit church nearly five-hundred metres away; the beautiful rendition of the choir came through the air like subtle waves, and it was nearly half an hour since I engrossed myself in another world.

19

I returned to the vicarage, with a heart reverberating with exultation. The phenomenon I witnessed in the intense moonlight raised my spirits to dizzying heights and the tower of faith, once in ruins, stood erect, scraping the clouds. Sagging shoulders straightened, the grief and anger which remained solidified in the heart vaporized in an instant. Apologetically, I threw myself at the feet of the vicar. With tearful eyes and beaming enthusiasm, he raised me up and hugged me.

The vicar returned the scriptures and the rosary abandoned by me a few weeks ago. That night, throughout, I lay on the bed pressing the divine objects to my bosom. Under tremendous exultation, my mind galloped like a horse, fear and uneasiness turned out to be the things of the past, and that night the scriptures and the rosary literally turned out to be my Kavacham and Kundalum (Armour and Earring).

The next day I took part in the morning prayers with the vicar and set out for a stroll after a sumptuous Christmas breakfast. I proceeded, conveying Christmas greeting to those who came to wish the elderly vicar. My enthusiasm rose manifold by the touch of the clear and cold morning. It appeared that the place had recouped its lost vigour; the tea gardens, the greens and the trees seemed thriving again.

I walked past the extensive green carpet of the tea gardens and stepped into the dense forest. The babbling of the brook came drifting through the air from afar. Suddenly a terrible scream emerged from the midst of the forest and close on its heels came a woman, from the depths of the jungle. She screamed desperately and charged at me with windswept hair and dishevelled, tattered clothes. She held something close to her chest as if taking care of an invaluable treasure. I shuddered at the fact that the woman charging towards me was none other than the queen of prostitutes. When she got closer, it became evident that she was charging as fast as a cheetah, with her son held close to her bosom, and it seemed her feet were hardly touching the ground because of the alarming speed. The ground stood thunderstruck on account of the anguished scream of the mother. The muscles on her face were taut under tremendous pressure. Like a wilted flower, her son rested on her chest. In a flash, I understood it was the child's ill health which had thrown her into a state of insanity. I snatched the child from her and held him close to my chest. It was absolutely like pressing hot coal onto the chest, and I wriggled in the great heat. The illness of the child was alarming and sent shivers through my heart.

Suddenly the child was thrown into convulsions. My limited knowledge of medicine acquired in connection with preparations for missionary work came in handy. To control the spiralling temperature of the child, I desperately searched for some water.

In the next instant, I found myself charging through the narrow winding forest tracks heading desperately for the brook. On account of urgency and seriousness of the situation, I was forced to throw caution to the winds, and run fast. In that desperate dash many twigs, leaves, thorns and stones got trampled under my feet. The mother of the child followed me closely, giving vent to heart-breaking cries.

We came very close to the stream, but with a shock my strides came to a grinding halt. I endured the feeling of my heart getting pierced by a knife. I dashed with the ailing child under immense stress, and mistakenly took an unknown track. As a result, we landed up in the most inaccessible gate to the stream. Right in front of us was the spot where the current plummeted to a depth of nearly a hundred metres and continued its journey through a gorge in the form of foamy waters. It was quite clear that even a little movement on my part could be fatal. Below us there was a platform of granite made by the rocks protruding into the gorge, with a crevice not large enough for a human being to pass through effortlessly.

The soul which slept on my chest suffered another convulsion. With a shudder I realized the fever was reaching highly alarming levels. I feared for the life of the child and shuddered at the possibility of his soul drifting away from us, like a leaf tossed in the wind. The only viable option that remained was to control the fever by drenching his body in the forest stream. Finally, I decided to take a plunge through the crevice for the sake of the suffering child. The smallest lapse could result in my body getting mutilated and shattered by the impact of crashing onto the rock. Since left with a Hobson's choice, I raised my eyes to the heaven for mustering courage and faith, then plunged into the air holding the ailing child firmly to my bosom. Suddenly my right shoulder became numb for a few seconds, and I found myself surrounded by foaming water. I grabbed the hair of the child who surfaced a few metres away, and then swam to the banks. I wrapped the feverish child in the wet shawl, and within seconds came his mother hurtling.

I kept on sponging his body with the wet shawl and struggled to extricate the child from the claws of convulsions. The contact with the wet shawl kept his body temperature in check. After providing this temporary relief to the ailing child, I sprang up and hurtled towards the church holding the child firmly to my chest. Blindly we ran past steep slopes, boulders and the tea gardens, and surmounted the challenges of the hostile terrain which was treacherous even at midday. Despite the deceptive nature of the landscape, my foot did not fumble, legs did not give way, because, the hand of my heavenly father held me tight.

We spotted a cart at the entrance of the church complex which was returning after unloading groceries at the vicarage. I threw myself violently into the cart with the ailing child and pulled his mother on board. The cart hurtled towards the hospital like lightning, swaying violently. I held the child firmly to my chest to protect him from flying away in the deadly dash of the cart.

I looked at the feminine soul, weeping beside me, and she looked fully devastated. In her eyes I failed to trace any fragments of lust; instead, it overflowed with the sorrow of a heartbroken mother. In amazing pace, the cart reached the hospital.

I struggled under the consuming pain on my right shoulder. While plunging into the current through the crevice the right shoulder scraped against the surface of granite. In the paroxysm of urgency, I remained totally unaware of the pain. I received first aid and left the hospital in the afternoon after confirming the appreciable progress in the condition of the child. I returned to the vicarage on foot and all through the walk prayed fervently for the well-being of the child. At every step the injury inflicted by the fall, throbbed and triggered ripples of pain. I even enjoyed the pain since the agony caused by the injury resulted in the survival of another soul. I considered the bruises suffered as the imprint of the divine, and daydreamed about the bestowal of many titles on me by heaven.

Within a few days the bruises I suffered healed in full. Through Devassy, I came to know about the return of the 'Queen of Prostitutes' and her son.

Despite being aware of the dangers that lurked in the forest, I ran at an alarming speed . . . why? I turned a blind eye and took an extremely dangerous plunge through the crevice, totally heedless of my safety . . . why? Despite thudding into the water, I could muster my senses and was able to tow the child to safety . . . how?

I have only one answer to these vexing questions. I found the 'divine' himself in the ailing child.

20

A few days after Christmas, one night, I experienced the most horrifying nightmare. I clearly saw a feminine image struggling to extricate itself from the unforgiving clutches of a treacherous mire. She screamed, wriggled, struggled and as a desperate attempt tried to raise an alarm by waving her hand. Her face looked convulsed with unbearable fear and agony. Finally, with an earth shattering scream, she drowned into the depths of the earth. I felt the ill-fated woman who had appeared in the dream had been none other than the 'Queen of Prostitutes', and the dream induced in me a fear for her welfare. I felt like the woman in the dreams she would also be swallowed by misfortune, and associated the waving of the hands in her final moments with the conveyance of the desperate distress signal—'save my soul'.

The next day I woke up with clear objectives. After the morning prayers with the vicar, I set off with determination, holding the scriptures close to my bosom. My confidence was bolstered under the unfailing shield of the Bible. I underwent the experience of inundation of joyful peace in the chambers of the heart. After reaching the faith home, I successfully persuaded Yohannan to get himself involved in the mission, then both of us proceeded towards the cave.

We proclaimed our arrival, standing at the entrance of the cave, in a loud voice. When the announcements failed to evoke any response, we peeped in and found the interior of the cave in a pathetic condition with utensils and clothes strewn all over the floor.

After ensuring that the cave was vacant, we withdrew from its vicinity.

We waded through the luxuriant, dense vegetation; undoubtedly we were under the influence of a strange force, and for the fulfilment of the divine mission, brushed all the hindrances aside and went ahead.

We reached the banks of the stream, which appeared like a silver band, and moved upstream. Not from afar came the roar of the waterfall that kept on intensifying at every step. We proceeded with steady steps and finally reached the waterfall, and were amazed at the plunge from a height of more than a hundred metres above us. Nature stood spellbound in the deep roar of the torrent. We scanned every nook and corner of the landscape for those two desperate souls, and found them finally, standing on higher grounds, very close to the falls.

Along the steep slopes, we climbed upwards overcoming the challenges of slippery rocks with careful and well-measured steps. On our right was the waterfall, which appeared to be woven with silver thread, and on the left stood dense vegetation. Suddenly the wind started gaining momentum, and the water drops flew in the air splitting seven colours from the light. The wind intensified as we climbed up. They were standing on a flatland, and the plunge of the current started nearly thirty metres above where they stood. After immense exertions against gravity, we reached closer but they remained fully unaware of our presence.

Suddenly the wind came to a halt, the plants stood motionless, and the roar of the fall overwhelmed every nook and corner of the landscape. With a shock, the woman, who was spreading out the washed clothes, turned back. Like a person with divine authority, I stepped forward and she turned pale on sighting us. With convulsions, she knelt down, and her gestures and body language reminded me of the woman in the New Testament who was destined to be pelted by stones.

I took a step forward. She started back and coiled herself like a serpent, and through her body language, which signalled immense fear, she sought forgiveness. Suddenly I trembled as if struck by lightning, and my body started overflowing with an invisible form of energy.

Shattering all restraints, the wind lashed the tall trees and the undergrowth shivered in fury. I placed my right palm on her head; her polluted body shivered as if struck by an unknown force, and she hissed and heaved a series of sighs. I raised the scriptures in my left hand and prayed to the Almighty from the bottom of my heart. Contrary to routine, throughout the prayer I kept my eyes open to witness the conveyance of messages from the Almighty through the medium of nature.

As mentioned in the 'Acts of the Apostles', the wind gained in intensity, the huge trees swayed like cane stems, and in the intensifying wind, I struggled to maintain balance. The shawl on my body unfolded like the wings of a mighty bird and remained buoyant. I opened the depths of the heart and prayed intensely, the divine ripples originating in me flowed into the woman, and my hand on her head acted as a channel for this process.

I raised my eyes to the heavens and found the tree tops oscillating wildly in the gush of air. The flakes of clouds got churned in the swirl of wind, and behind them appeared the radiance of the sun.

I prayed for the purification of her extremely polluted body and soul, which had been polluted by thousands. Yohannan stayed close to me and glorified the deeds of the Almighty in prayers. The tottering tall trees appeared like the provoked crowd who wanted to pelt the fallen woman with stones.

In the intense wind, the plunging stream of water changed its course and the particles of vapour flew in the air obscuring the surroundings often. I prayed for the cleansing of her soul which was as filthy as Augean stables. At the pinnacle of the prayer, she shuddered, shivered and spun like a pivoted top. Her restrained sobs turned into tears, and I clearly felt the warmth of the tears carrying the smell of blood stains.

We continued praying for her, the strange phenomenon encircled us, and gradually narrowed its radius. Towering trees with an air of invincibility suddenly looked vulnerable to the forces of nature. They swayed, tottered and even struggled to maintain their footing on the forest bed. The undergrowth and bushes were almost ripped off from the roots. In the pinnacle of prayer, at its zenith, my body gave a start as if struck by lightning and the aftershocks radiated into the mortal image of the condemned soul. A sharp but short note of scream emerged from her.

She slammed into the ground violently as impacted by something unearthly. That very moment, it came to my realization that the 'Queen of Prostitute' no longer carries that title. The cloud flakes madly hovering over us scattered and vanished. Gradually the wind started to ease and finally died down. The flora regained stability, the thin veil of moisture vanished and nature returned to normalcy.

She sat on the ground, with our support. Like comforting his sister who is in distress, Yohannan held her close to his chest. Slowly, she came back to her senses and presented a short sketch of her past. Her name was Susanna, and she hailed from a middle-class family. At the onset of her adolescence, unknowingly and unthinkingly, she had plummeted into the filthy abyss of carnal sins. On losing her parents as well as the property, she was forced to accept flesh trade in order to scrape a living. At the end of the narrative, like the sudden burst of dammed up current, she burst into tears. Her tears corroded and burnt our hearts. Since she was born and brought up in a religious environment, she used to cherish golden memories about the services in the church. Compelled by an irresistible urge, she ventured to view the church services on Sundays from afar, under the cover of vegetation. In fact, what she revealed unlocked the enigma I had encountered in the form of an apparition that had appeared through the gaps of swaying bushes while delivering a sermon at the lectern on the altar.

'Are you still so keen on attending church service?' I asked. She nodded in the affirmative, pouring out her unquenchable thirst for the divine. Then I instructed Susanna to come to the church at ten o'clock in the morning, the following day. We were about to return, and before leaving I told her in a strict voice, 'Never ever sin again.'

The next day, in the morning, after the prayers, armed with the scriptures I proceeded to the church and settled at the facade of the church. In order to provide the most ideal backdrop for the impending noble event, the Almighty presented to me the most salubrious forms of nature. That morning had the ideal blend of a nip and warmth. The extensive green shone like a carpet studded with countless emeralds.

I unfolded the scriptures. Unveiled before me was the gospel of John. The crowd drags in a woman accused of adultery before Christ for judgement. They wanted to get the expert opinion of Christ regarding the enforceability of the law of Moses which prescribes pelting to death for an adulterous person. Jesus commands, 'Let the person who is sinless among you cast the first stone.'

Heavily laden with embarrassment, the crowd melted away one by one. Jesus says to the adulteress, 'I am not judging you . . . go and never ever sin again.'

The message triggered ripples in my heart. It became evident that what we had witnessed the day before near the waterfall had a striking parallel with the incident recounted in the scriptures. I thanked the Almighty for making me instrumental in the transformation of Susanna.

I raised my head at the soft footfalls on the lawn and found two shadows stretching towards me. Drifting towards the facade of the church were Susanna and her son. With a beating heart, I proceeded to the steps. It was quite evident that they were walking in profound reluctance. In the light breeze the edges of her sari and the headgear fluttered gently. They stopped near the steps of the facade and raised her tearful eyes at me with folded arms. Her eyes shone like pearls with intense gratitude.

Slowly, I placed the scriptures in her palm and with shivering hands she held it close to her bosom. I guided her into the sanctified interiors of the church. Slowly she ascended the steps and moved through the smooth granite floor. Then she set her right foot into the church, and in the height of exultation her body fluttered like a string.

She swayed on account of the blend of excitement and apprehension. With unsteady steps, she moved to the altar through the aisle, then threw herself down near the altar and prayed. The prayer turned out to be a long one, and throughout the meditation she held the scriptures firmly close to her bosom.

21

Throughout the days after Christmas service, the vicar remained buoyant; the positive changes exhibited in my manner raised his hopes sky high. With a positive body language and gestures, he threw himself into the hectic schedule of parish activities.

We were only a few hours away from the stroke of midnight which would herald the onset of the New Year. The congregation braced themselves up for the Watch Night Service and Holy Communion, and the believers flocked in great numbers to the church that was basking in the radiance of hundreds of flames. The church was packed well before the commencement of Watch Night Service. With boundless optimism and anticipation the multitude stood facing the altar.

The initial phase of the Service commenced, and the walls of the church echoed the Gregorian chant of the vicar. The congregation stood spellbound in the resonance; the atmosphere in the church got saturated with the music, and the renditions of the choir came forth in the form of melodious notes.

A few minutes before midnight, candles were distributed all over the church, and they will came alive at the stroke of midnight hour. All the flames in and around the church complex got extinguished, and the interior of the church turned dark except for the little flame left on the altar.

We were at the threshold of the New Year; with bated breath and in absolute silence the congregation waited to ring in the new. Exactly at midnight the vicar lighted another candle from the unextinguished flame at the altar, with prayers and humility I accepted it, and turned towards the congregation. In the insufficient illumination the congregation appeared like an extensive sea of black.

Shielding the flame with the left palm, with measured steps I moved towards the congregation and lighted the candles of the volunteers who came forth from the congregation. I handed the flame back to the vicar, and he infused life into the lamps on the pedestal. Gradually the altar turned golden.

The flame-bearing volunteers infused radiance onto the candles held by the first row of believers and from the slight elevation of the altar, I observed with curiosity the permeation of the radiance through the length and breadth of the church.

The congregation appeared before me as a human body and the streaks of radiance crisscrossing the huge mass of people appeared as the breath of life breathed into the nostrils of the mortals by the Almighty. The pulsation of life in the form of radiance appeared coursing through the veins of the congregation and within a few moments the radiance stretched all over the church. It seemed the congregation was throbbing with life, and the believers bearing the flame looked like a celestial army.

A tiny flame lighted from the altar turned into hundreds and thousands in a flash like the spewing of the legendary bow Gandeevam described in the Mahabharata and I concluded with certainty the possibility of righteousness proliferating into hundreds, thousands and millions like the tiny flame on the altar. The phenomenal growth of the radiance through the length and breadth of the congregation appeared to leave an everlasting impression on my mind. I yearned to associate myself with the tiny flame I had accepted from the vicar and became desirous of conveying the unparalleled love of the Almighty to every nook and corner of human habitation by consoling the sorrowful, curing the sick and conveying the boundless love of the Almighty.

The Watch Night Service and the Holy Communion spanned many hours; the vicar bestowed the sacramental wine and bread to the congregation that knelt before the altar. His commitment to the Almighty appeared profound doubtlessly, and like a youngster beaming with energy he kept on moving from one end of the altar to the other to serve the sacraments to the congregation. In worship the vicar appeared as one untouched by thirst, hunger, ailments and weariness, and his body turned itself into an everlasting source of vigour. I craved to emulate his example.

We returned to the vicarage in the morning after the conclusion of Watch Night Service and associated formalities; after the breakfast I stretched myself into the bed for a nap, and in a flash the nap turned into a deep slumber.

To my amazement, the vicar knocked me up from sound sleep and offered an invitation for a forenoon stroll in the vicinity of the church. Since an invitation for a stroll with the vicar was the rarest of the rare occasion, I got up disregarding the weariness.

In the most beautiful, clear forenoon laced with a healthy, gentle nip, I held the vicar's hand and helped him to move parallel to the church. Walking past the church complex, traversing the extensive frontyard carpeted with grass, we reached near the short wall bordering the tea gardens. We sat on the wall; the vicar appeared beaming on that beautiful forenoon and I turned my focus on the beautiful landscape extending up to the horizons.

'Dear Child.'

I responded to the voice of the vicar overflowing with affection by refocusing my gaze on him. 'This is the sixty-fifth year of my priesthood.'

I was amazed at the decades-long tenure of the vicar as the servant of the Almighty and he stood like a huge tree laden with the profusion of fruits in the orchard of the divine.

The vicar hails from an illustrious family in Kuttanad, born to a wealthy merchant and his palatial ancestral home stands on the tributary of River Pampa near a large berthing place for traditional boats. The vicar used the analogy of the ancient port of Muziris to draw a clear sketch of the bustling commercial activities in the berth near the ancestral home. The berth used to accommodate hundreds of boats, and resembled a beehive throughout the day, teaming with activities, standing testimony to the glory of his father in commerce.

He came to know the Almighty from the pearls of scriptures scattered from the lips of his mother; even at the first reference about the Messiah he came under the influence of the magnetism of the Christ, and accepted priesthood ignoring the severe opposition from his father. In other words, the vicar had been in pursuit of the Almighty who walked on the earth curing the sick, raising the dead and calming the wrath of nature.

'I have pursued the Almighty for many years.'

It seemed the vicar was on the verge of raising the narration to a higher level, and my curiosity was like a ship with sail unfolded.

'Finally after crossing seventy . . . I was bestowed with the rare privilege.'

My body straightened up; with pounding heart I focused fully on the vicar.

'I have not been able to see him with naked eyes . . . but have seen his reflection . . . I clearly witnessed how he consoled the deprived, and how he embraced the marginalized.'

The vicar seemed overwhelmed by powerful emotion, his voice sounded powerful, and the body appeared broken the bondage of weariness.

Furthering my curiosity, the narration of the vicar turned the clock back by a decade and a half. Fifteen years back, in the month of August, the south west monsoon slammed onto the heights with unprecedented intensity, and many aborigine settlements remained cut off from the outside world for many weeks. When the azure of the sky returned the news of an aborigine settlement under the grip of severe contagious diseases reached the vicar, and pushed his uneasiness to unbearable levels. He decided to visit the settlement with relief and provisions.

To ease off the burden of negotiating the hostile terrain with a sackful of provisions and medicines, the vicar requested Tresa's household for a draught animal, and they responded enthusiastically by arranging five horses laden with sackfuls of food packets, water, medicines and clothing. Tresa, along with her father, volunteered for the journey with the vicar to the depths of the forest to carry the provisions to the impoverished aborigine settlements, and the trio left on a clear morning when the weather looked conducive.

'Those days the roar of the waterfall sounded like the roar of many waters mentioned in the Book of Revelations,' recollected the vicar.

They traversed the streams conveying powerful torrents, moved through the midst of thousands of springs sprouting like volcanoes, and on account of heavy falls the forest tracks appeared impassable. Surmounting these adversities with sturdy determination the trio inched towards the ill fated aborigine settlement, and succeeded in reaching the destination before noon.

In a flash the trio plunged themselves into the cumbersome relief activities, the inhabitants of the settlement engulfed them like moths to a flame and many souls who were reduced to mere bags of bones pleaded profusely even for a few crumbs of bread.

The vicar paused for a moment, his eyes turned tearful and the variations in his expressions symbolized the powerful emotions he was undergoing. At amazing pace, the relief efforts started progressing, the food packets and medicines were handed out and after an interlude of a fortnight from the aborigine settlement started issuing the curls of smoke. Tresa treated the people whose bodies were mottled with scars and abscess. She wiped off the pus of the ailing with her own hand on account of the limited quantity of gauze and cotton.

'Till then I had remained oblivious of the most difficult dimension of spirituality, receiving the abhorrence and secretions of others on our own body,' testified the vicar.

An elderly aborigine woman who was in a precarious condition required urgent medical attention and the trio decided to take her to the hospital for better treatment. They reassured and emboldened the inhabitants by promising more provisions and relief in the following days, and returned to the heights with the ailing woman after prayers.

22

The task of carrying the elderly ailing woman turned out to be extremely difficult; a special bed of bamboo poles was improvised for her. After rolling out a thatched mat on the bed, the ailing woman was stretched on it and four youngsters from the settlement came forward volunteering to carry the bed through the uneven forest tracks.

They made their way through the treacherous forest bed with careful and precise steps.

In the afternoon the vast expanse of clouds from the west came rushing towards the heights unexpectedly, and rolled out the envelope of dimness over the forest bed. The vicar and Tresa threw uneasy upward glances at regular intervals exhibiting apprehensions. Suddenly a blazing streak of lightning crisscrossed the horizon and close on its heels arrived a loud clap of thunder. The army of clouds drew arrows from their rich quavers, stretched out the strings of their mighty bows and launched millions of arrows of Lord Varuna. The thick canopy of the forest swayed in the lashing wind, and the goddess of vegetation intercepted the raining of arrows with the shield of green. The intensity of the rain grew and in the space of a snap millions of moist harpoons hurtled towards the earth. The arrows of Lord Varuna percolating through the gaps in the green canopy scratched the skin of the returning relief team with their freezing tips of moisture.

To protect the ailing elderly woman from the ruthless and relentless attack of nature, the relief team took an abrupt turn from their designated path and forged ahead under the guidance of aborigine youngsters. They were heading for an ideal haven capable of providing a cover over their head and a screen around them that would protect them from the cruelties of nature. The relief team negotiated a thickly wooded steep slope and headed for the ultimate destination on top of the hill totally unknown to the outside world. In the steep ascent the aborigine youngsters struggled considerably to keep the ailing from swaying and shaking.

The woods started to thin out with the progression of the climb and gradually gave way to grass swaying madly in the wind; traversing the waist deep grass, surmounting the steepness of the slope and battling the battering raindrops they reached the summit of the hill.

Despite the dimness and thick festoons of raindrops the huge accumulation of granite at the summit of the hill drew the attention of the vicar. They were in the ruins of a huge ancient temple and found refuge in a stone structure with a roof made of granite and with pillars supporting the roof which could be turned into perfect poles to restrain the horses.

The winds gained intensity, the raindrops pierced into the land, and constant flashes of lightning helped the relief team to orientate themselves at frequent intervals. In a short spasm of lightning the relief team found a chamber made of stone at one end of the structure and snuggled themselves into it for safety.

Even in the midst of darkness and uncertainties Tresa stayed close to the ailing and tried to ease her discomfort through incessant nursing coated with affection. All of them remained in the chamber struggling to catch a glimpse of the surroundings in the short flashes of lighting, and sat on the cold granite floor waiting for the hours of darkness to pass.

With the passage of time the ice-cold granite floor infused discomfort in the vicar with muscle cramps, and he felt as though an invisible force was trying to tear the legs apart. The awareness of being stranded in the temple in the depth of the forest intensified his apprehensions and contributed significantly to the discomfort. The incessant rains, howling winds and the series of lightning and thunder furthered his fear.

By the streaks of lightning the vicar assessed the positions of members of the relief team in the chamber, and found the youngsters seated near the door, Tresa's father next to him and Treasa at the farthest corner with the ailing on her lap.

The vicar struggled under the discomfort which was growing every moment and was able to find a short spell of slumber only after midnight. An earth-shattering thunder knocked him up from the light slumber. Suddenly the interior of the chamber blazed under an intense lightning and the vicar caught a glimpse of a sight that shook him to the core. He found someone with heavenly grace nursing the ailing in the place of Tresa. The apparition with golden long hair, sparkling eyes and the grace of a thousand solar flares left permanent imprint in the mind of the vicar. With a pounding heart he waited impatiently for the next spasm of lightning. When the interiors of the chamber shone under an intense lightning the vicar quickly threw a glance towards where Tresa sat, with hope and anxiety to reconfirm the vision of the one with heavenly grace, and found Tresa holding the ailing to her bosom. Her golden hairs still carried the imprint of kisses given by nature in the form of raindrops. The phenomenon of Tresa, who provided comfort to the elderly woman by radiating the warmth of her bosom despite the adverse circumstances, astonished the vicar profoundly and he tried to write off what he witnessed a few moments back as a mere aberration of a weary mind.

Again fear surfaced in the vicar like a poisonous serpent with expanded hood, and in response he stretched on the granite floor with eyes closed. The battering of raindrops went on uninterrupted, the fluttering of branches of the trees echoed in the ears, the ruins of the temple shuddered under the clap of thunder.

Slowly and gradually came the soothing arms of a cool breeze dispelling stress from the mind and the heart, and the vicar fluttered in an ecstasy similar to what he experienced whenever he stepped into the church. He enjoyed an unearthly peace on that night in the midst of overwhelming turbulence, akin to what he experienced whenever he prayed at the altar. The vicar doubtlessly testified to the presence of his Lord in the ruins of the ancient temple.

With the passage of time the turbulence of nature turned music to the ears of the vicar, the swaying treetops sounded like the dance steps of monsoon, the cracking of thunder emerged as the rhythm of nature and the dazzle of lightning appeared as the glittering outfit of a celestial dancer. The turbulence turned melodious for the vicar and in that beautiful melody of nature he slowly drifted into deep sleep.

The vicar paused for a while, and his tale was nearing its end. The warmth of the sunbeams and the gentle nip in the wind churned out a rare magic potion which infused boundless enthusiasm in us.

I narrowed down my focus on the vicar and found his gaze transfixed solely on me. His eyes appeared overflowing with enthusiasm and it seemed he wanted to give a fitting conclusion to his narrative. With heightened curiosity I retained my gaze on him without a wink.

'Child . . . do you know where exactly in the temple we found refuge and shelter that night?'

With this question he raised me to the incredible heights of curiosity. I responded with a shake of the head that conveyed my lack of awareness in this matter.

Then, with considerable excitement the vicar whispered in my ears, 'Exactly in the middle of Grabhagriham.'

23

The words whispered by the vicar held me spellbound; sensing the presence of our Lord in the sanctum of a dilapidated temple turned out to be something beyond my imagination even in my wildest dreams.

The vicar continued, 'It has been an eye-opener for me and my pursuit of Christ came to a successful conclusion that night. I clearly witnessed the deeds of Christ through the kind gestures of Tresa.'

'That night I came to grips with the greatest truth of all times . . . it is impossible to regionalize or localize the Almighty. The Supreme Being is omnipotent, omnipresent and omniscient.'

'We all are the children of the power who is the alpha and the omega. All are the children of the Almighty,' the vicar added, In the late hours of the night, the rain eased, the wind subsided and after a while the streaks of dawn appeared in the horizon. The faint rays of light slowly squeezed into the interiors of the Garbhagriham, and the vicar scanned the chamber in the faint light. Only Tresa remained awake nursing the ailing as if nursing a child, and the ailing slept like an infant on her lap.

A faint touch of red appeared in the eastern horizon and in the mist-induced faintness, the inquisitive vicar started to encircle the vast expanse of the temple ruins. Growing curiosity prompted him to turn a blind eye to the needling chill, turn a deaf ear to the awakening sonorousness of the wild, and with feeble steps he waded through the earth turned slippery in the overnight rain.

The accumulation of mist, that stood like an envelope on the vast expanse of ruins, started to thin out in the emerging sunbeams. Slowly but in steady pace the penetrating sharpness of sunbeams diluted the cover of the mist and brought out the outlines of the archaeological marvel. The gradual dilution of fog revealed the enormity of the ruins much to the astonishment of the vicar.

Despite the cessation of the rains, the air remained saturated with moisture. The land on which the foundation of the temple was based appeared like a plateau on top of the lofty hill, and the fringes of the plateau had been lined with tall trees. Gradually the sunbeams strengthened, bringing out the intricate details of the ruin, with pillars and the carved images protruding.

The marvel unravelled by nature held the vicar in utter amazement. It must have been a huge structure centuries back, and one wonders what would have prompted men to raise such a large structure on top a hill which is nearly inaccessible even now. The efforts expended and logistics needed for bringing the huge blocks of stones turned out to be absolutely mind boggling. That moment, the vicar realized that what lay in the form of an accumulation of stones used to be a place of worship of immense significance. With reasonable knowledge in history and archaeology, the vicar dated the ruins in the vicinity of 500 AD.

With racing heart and unsteady footsteps the vicar stepped into the midst of the ruins. Even upon the first footfall, the vicar experienced something akin to the passage of electricity through his feet that radiated all over his body. For a moment he stood in the pinnacle of marvel which reminded him of the breathtaking experiences he enjoyed within the four walls of the church. With a pounding heart he waded through the stone boulders that carried the weather-beaten images of the carvings. The mist had thinned out.

The vicar stood in disbelief at the sights emerging from the withdrawing mist. Millions of stones, thousands of carvings, hundreds of dilapidated pillars that once supported heavy granite roofs. The foundations of many chambers, many walls half ruined, and steps at regulars intervals coated with moss. The sunbeams strengthened, the haze enveloping the valleys melted away and from the vanishing haze emerged the eastern slopes of the Western Ghats coated with the radiance of the sunlight. From the ruins the vicar threw a glance into the plains beyond the eastern valleys of the ranges that appeared like a brown canopy dotted with green patches of vegetation.

'I examined closely the carvings on the stones and pillars, and pieced together the illegible images and became delighted to find the peaceful coexistence of Aryan and Dravidian figures on it,' said the vicar. Then he continued: 'I could clearly visualize the temple in all its glory thousands of years back. I could see the congregation worshipping, irrespective of Aryan or Dravidian. From the fragments of the structure strewn all over, I found the evidence of a great nation where people all lived in equality, devoid of evil and injustice and where lies and false accusations were totally unheard of. I remained fully immersed in that period when my nation was at the pinnacle of its glory.'

I sat in front of the vicar, totally speechless. Right before my eyes he tore down with authority the walls of religious dissension, caste and creed.

'Suddenly I felt like prophet Nehemiah who wailed for the walls of Jerusalem in ruins. His heart pounded for his nation; likewise, I wept for the abode of the Almighty that was in ruins, I cried for our nation and the great culture which was also in ruins. My heart pulsated for the restoration of the glory of my nation and the pride of the people. Thousands of our brethren suffer from poverty, exploitation, illness and lack of education. Dear child . . . I believe you are the torchbearer . . . go and serve the people, let your love transcend the barriers of caste, colour, creed and religion.'

I remained dumbfounded, confused to the core.

On gauging my confused mind, the vicar cried, 'You have the attestation of the scriptures . . . I can prove it.'

Suddenly the vicar rose, beckoned me to follow him and with swift steps walked across the extensive front yard of the church. I remained stupefied at the strange mannerism and the haste, in spite of being in the prime of youth I struggled to keep pace with him. I had no idea where he was heading for; with a slight stoop he kept on forging ahead, and at times made me run to keep abreast of the frail old vicar.

The brisk footsteps of the vicar culminated in the facade of the church; he placed his right hand on the large door and slowly the doors gave way with a prolonged screech. The vicar stepped into the interiors of the church half illuminated by the beams of light percolating through the glass tiles on the roof. I stayed right behind him, and again with brisk steps he proceeded to the altar. That forenoon the vicar seemed like an abundant source of energy, he stepped onto the elevated lectern and gestured me to stand facing the altar.

My curiosity hovered high at the strange gesticulations of the vicar, and it seemed he wanted to convey something of immense significance to me. The vicar kept his hands on the pulpit Bible with profound reverence, turned the pages and focused on a chapter; then he raised his face and focused his gaze on me. Standing on the elevated lectern he appeared like a divine archer on a chariot driven by the Almighty yearning to launch arrows on the powers of evil and his face bore the expression of utmost seriousness.

In a flash, with the aid of a few Malayalam words, he transported me back to the first century of the Christian era and replanted me in the ancient port city of Joppa in Israel. The vicar spoke not through words but in images, and in the faint illumination of the interiors of the church, Peter, the prominent disciple of Christ emerged before my eyes. I literally witnessed his graceful ascent to the rooftop for prayer; gradually he turned weary on account of hunger, and in prayer drifted into a trance.

I witnessed a sudden gush of energy from the vicar that emerged in the form of a powerful sermon. Every word flew at me like arrows, pierced my heart, and left everlasting impressions of the Almighty. Instead of the frail shaking voice, I heard the roar of an ocean in the faintly illuminated interiors of the church, the voice of the vicar emerged in the form of waves and reverberated within the four walls.

Like a skilled artist the vicar painted the image of Peter drifting into slumber with the outline of words and colours scooped from the palette of scriptures. Then slowly the vicar unfolded the vision experienced by Peter while he plunged into the bottom of trance. I really witnessed the lowering of a great sheet knit at four corners from heaven, found all kinds of quadrupeds on the earth, all kinds of reptiles crawling on and beneath the surface, and all birds of the air. I heard their roar, baying, bleating, neighing, barking, and chirping vividly, and shivered at the voice of the Almighty descended from heaven commanding Peter to rise, kill and eat.

I clearly made out the wavering of Peter and his subsequent denials.

'Lord I can't do that! I have never eaten anything that is unclean and not fit for consumption.'

I clearly heard the voice of the Almighty that sounded like the roar of thunder.

'When God says that something is clean, that is not unclean.'

This happened three times and finally the sheet with animals vanished into the dizzying heights of the sky.

For a moment an uneasy silence took over the interiors of the church, and the gaze of the vicar remained transfixed on me. Then the vicar continued.

'The message of the Almighty got engraved deeply onto the heart of Peter. The Lord accepts men from all the nations who fear him and do what is right. The Almighty opened the eyes of Peter that were blindfolded by mere Jewishness. Likewise we all need to open our eyes blindfolded by the band of caste, creed and religion.'

Another short spell of silence unfolded in the church. The vicar who bore the tint of an unearthly authority on the face slowly raised his right hand, pointed the index finger at me and commanded, 'Child ... this is your mission—tear down the walls of segregation and serve the people in the name of the Lord. The scripture says there is only one god and all are his children irrespective of caste, creed, sex, race and religion.'

His unusually powerful voice reverberated in the church and under its lashings the pigeons resting on the ceiling fluttered their wings and flew away.

Like Moses who witnessed the burning bush on Mount Sinai, I stood bewildered and numb at the magnitude of the mission entrusted onto my shoulders.

24

The once majestic peak turned colourless and dull; in the intensity of summer the green canopy of the slopes looked worn out and even the wildlife in the vicinity of the heights reeled under the impact of the scorching heat.

Suddenly came a soothing breeze, under its influence the temperature slided down to bearable levels; close on its heels came drifting a heavenly melody that electrified the peaks, steep slopes and the valleys.

The golden hair cascading in the air . . . the landscape basked in the radiance of that angel, and with heavenly beauty she ascended the steep slopes of the mountain. At the touch of her feet the landscape turned green, flowers blossomed, the atmosphere became aromatic and the valleys and slopes appeared repainted with green. The landscape turned emerald-green and the flora throbbed with a new lease of life. Finally she reached the summit; the clouds that rushed forth to wrap her turned radiant crowning the peak with gold.

I rose under the influence of the beautiful dream; after prayer and breakfast I bade adieu to Esteppan, and proceeded to the summit of the peak. I felt the presence of a treasure at the summit throbbing for my presence to reveal something of essence.

The sunlight was mild in the morning and through the semi-transparency of the mist I enjoyed the beauty and aroma of the creeper covering the tomb. The aroma and beauty of the flowers acted as motivators for me to go ahead with the difficult mission, and with prayers I walked past the church complex and then headed for the forest.

Through the hostile forest tracks, I moved with energy and vigour. Out of heightened excitement my heart pounded like a drum, and as a result, the roar of the waterfall sounded not very attractive that day.

I emerged out of the forest and stepped onto the extensive grassland, and in its boundless expanse stood the peak afar, head held high. Like an emperor on a conquest to capture the four corners of the world, I trampled down the grass and moved forward. In the growing sunlight, I set up my mind to enjoy the mild emotions of nature.

Suddenly there appeared a strange phenomenon in the horizon, and upon the advancement of the strange apparition of nature that was as high as the canopy of the sky, even the towering peak was partly hidden. It marched onto me challenging the radiance of the sun, and I remained stupefied at the unseen face of the fog that charged at me like an army of millions. I placed my faith in God, stood firm with head high, ready to challenge the might of the phenomenon.

It crashed onto me like a wave and under its impact my body arched backwards, the grass blades rippled in strong winds, and like the tentacles of an octopus the arms of the fog entangled me firmly. The initial gust of wind eased, eventually died down, and in the poor light I advanced with utmost care. I faintly heard the chanting of evil mantras in the mist, and it sounded as repulsive as the scraping of a snake in the sand. The thick veil of the mist made my movement sluggish, and with much effort I reached the base of the peak suffering the sting of thousands of needles in the swirling chilly wind.

Standing at the base of the peak, I threw an upward glance and found only the grey canopy of the sky. The ascent turned exceedingly hard, but I remained undaunted by the dangers posed by the climb. With the sturdy determination to set foot on the summit to unravel the mysteries, I kept on forging ahead.

The ascent began, and I experienced the feeling of the Almighty guiding upwards, holding my arms, enabling me to advance tearing away the thick sheets of challenges. On the previous journey with Yohannan to the summit, gravity was the sole opponent, but the second time it turned out to be the allied attack of gravity, mist and wind. They unleashed their lethal attack relentlessly on me from three different fronts. The faith in God which strengthened me acted as an unfailing shield and aided me in the battle with the forces of nature. Like a skilled sword fighter of 'Kalari', I could evade the 'Othiram' and 'Poozhi Kadakam' of the adversities.

I inched forward through the thick curtain of mist, at times crawling and creeping; the murmur and chant of slight drizzle tried to distract my mind that focused only on God, and I struggled to maintain the balance through the almost vertical slopes. The awareness of the dangers a false step could cause intensified my concentration. The impact of the wind which carried a sharp knife edge made the task more and more daunting. In fact, I ascended not by sight, but because of faith.

I wrestled with the forces of nature for many hours, then started negotiating another steep slope, turning, twisting and at times snaking, making progress at a snail's pace. The mist kept on intensifying and to save myself from the howling wind I crept upwards like reptiles, and scraping against the rough surface scratched my skin. The thickness of the fog also tried to push me downwards, but my faith in God made the fighting spirit in me come alive and kept me going. Suddenly I encountered the feeling of standing on flat ground, and this prompted me to dart forward tearing the resistance of lashing wind and fog. Then I experienced a miracle.

Shoots of greenery sprouted before me and I found the summit of the peak a few meters afar. In the depths of declivity drifted the ocean of milk over the terrain I surmounted. Panting like a dog, I threw myself on the emerald green near the summit. My heart beat fast on account of the ascent.

Suddenly, there came from the summit a gust of wind lashed with rumbling and I jumped up, shocked.

In a flash, it hurtled down, a strange sight to witness, and the wind with sharp edges sliced the fog that had enveloped the steep slopes of the peak, exposing the path I scaled. The cloud flakes scattered all over like cotton flakes blown by the gust; slowly the clouds transformed themselves into walls, and remained on both sides of the peak. I witnessed what was cited in the Book of Exodus, the appearance of clouds as walls. The sun emerged through the semi-transparency of the mist, and the pillar of clouds formed and reformed with the movement of the wind. In one instant, it assumed the shape of a pillar, in the next instant, appeared as a blanket.

Through the corner of the eye, I witnessed the emergence of a strange phenomenon exactly at the summit, and with a start I fixed my gaze at the unusual occurrence. Like an erected obelisk emerged a pillar of clouds, and with careful steps I moved forward to observe the event closely. Right in front of me a treasure of divinity started revealing itself, the pillar of clouds started to thin out and in the gentle breeze the pristine blades of grass rippled.

Slowly, with measured steps, I approached the summit, and the phenomenon gradually assumed a human shape. My heart pounded on account of an inexplicable joy . . . I was only a few yards away from the summit. Golden hair cascading in the wind . . . the loose garments fluttering in the gentle breeze . . . I saw the unearthly beauty clearly, her eyes shone like a nebula, when she smiled I underwent an experience that was akin to the passage of electricity. The face I had seen many years back reappeared in heavenly grace, her beautiful eyes remained transfixed on me, affection and compassion overflowed from her face. I almost reached the summit; the unearthly apparition of Tresa remained at an arm's length. Gradually, her arms started spreading out, and under the influence of a strange force I raised my hands involuntarily and enjoyed the heavenly bliss of her touch that fully uprooted evil from my heart.

Suddenly, there emerged a halo with the radiance of countless solar flares, and the apparition of Tresa was eclipsed under its glory. I vividly felt my hands being gripped by someone who is divine to the core. I struggled to keep my eyelids peeled; with difficulty I turned my gaze onto the arms holding me, and found clearly the impressions of nail marks on the palm. My heart galloped like a horse, and in total disorientation I bowed down at the feet of the halo that appeared extending to the four corners of the universe. My eyes, in uncontrollable ecstasy, read the nail marks of the feet. With immense struggle, I raised my eyes and found the palms with the nail marks lowering from the sky; it came down in pursuit of me and eventually raised and pressed me to its bosom. I experienced a celestial bliss that transported me to paradise.

Finally, I surfaced from the depths of the celestial bliss, and there appeared before me the landscape devoid fully of any molecules of mist. My heart and mind overflowed with heavenly joy. Through a powerful prayer surfaced from the inmost depths of my heart, I thanked the Almighty and under its influence even the mighty ranges of the Western Ghats stood in awe.

25

The untimely summer rains unfolded the thick canopy of clouds over the heights, and the gates of heaven remained open for a week. In the incessant rains, the ground turned more luxuriant and thousands of springs sprouted in the forest. On the peaks, innumerable channels of running water appeared, and the roar of the waterfall amplified tenfold. It had the bearings of a divine plan, for staging a significant event.

I turned all the days soaked in rain into days of prayer and tried to surrender myself before the Supreme Being. Consequently, the chambers of my heart filled with an inexplicable joy. Prayers channelled the flow of the divine forces into me, and the melody of the raindrops set a perfect backdrop for my interaction with the divine.

On certain occasions, I prayed and meditated over the scriptures near the facade of the church, and the festoons of raindrops, streaming from the slanting roof made the settings more florid. I ascended to the higher levels of spirituality in the melody of rains, and the tiny fragments of moisture that flew past me left a pleasurable chill on my face.

Finally, the doors of the heavens closed, the intense azure of the sky reappeared and in the bright sunlight the place looked more beautiful. Within a few days, illuminated by bright sunbeams, the strange unique mosaic of nature appeared in the grassland. The neelakurunji flowers, which bloom in perfect cycles of twelve years, blossomed untimely in large numbers,.

The grasslands and valley turned into sparkling beds of sapphire, the blaze of flowers fascinated the residents of the heights and prompted many from different corners of the country to visit and witness this rare event. The mesmerizing fragrance of flowers, the invigorating, salubrious weather and the gold-coated sunrays turned the heights into an absolute feast for the eyes. From the deep forests came the winds carrying the medicinal value of rare herbs that made the air extremely pure and healthy. Indeed, the heights braced itself up for the footfall of the Almighty, and the myriad colours showered from the palette of nature bathed the landscape in unrivalled beauty.

Backed by incessant prayers, I embarked on a series of mission activities which started with the rehabilitation of Susanna and her child. With the boundless support received from the parish, and above all the blessings showered from heaven, we could complete the mission with resounding success. Susanna got employed by one of the institutions of the mother church, and her son received admission into one of the schools managed under the auspices of the parish.

We enjoyed those joyful days when our creative efforts remained at their best. Throughout those days, Yohannan extended overwhelming support to me, and every cell in us throbbed with the elements of the divine. We tried to channel the power descended from heaven towards the paths of creativity, and immersed ourselves fully in the activities of the mission caring nothing for the satisfaction of our basic needs like thirst, hunger, clothing and comfort. For radiating the unparalleled love of Jesus, we traversed the mountains, hills, dense forests, and trampled on the rocks and thorns. We explored the innermost depths of the forest where animals roam without an iota of fear. The divine vision I experienced at the summit fully effaced fear from the depths of my heart.

With relentless efforts, we tried to reach out to the remote corners of the heights, consoled the souls disfigured by ailments by holding them to our bosom, and with joy served our fellow men and women. Wherever we visited we scattered the diamonds, gems and pearls of the gospel abundantly; thousands of souls could smile for the first time in their lives, and people from all religious backgrounds approached and offered us their support. We remained united without the label of any religion; we worked without the banner of any sect, and we the children of the Almighty worked untiringly. We had only one religion . . . the religion of love, and we loved one another. Everyone in the heights upheld us in their prayers, and their blessings acted as shields, protecting us in the fight against adversities.

Nature also supported us by staying congenial. We enjoyed the gentle, soothing touch of the breeze, and with soft, gentle hands the breeze caressed the extensive flower beds which in turn responded with ripples of colour. The sun saved us from weariness by emitting only lukewarm beams, and the air of the heights saturated with the smell of flowers made us energetic. The Almighty seemed to have set his foot on the land which blazed with the colours of thousands of different flowers. We held the heart-broken, and showered consoling words on them, the power of prayer cured many souls, and thousands enjoyed the warmth of love and affection which had been unknown to them in the past. The seeds of the gospel we scattered in the heights sprouted and yielded fruit for many a soul.

During this time, another miracle unfolded in the cemetery. The creeper that obscured the tomb of Tresa lengthened its countless arms amazingly and stretched to all directions like streaks of lightning. It stretched itself up to the walls of the cemetery piercing through many headstones; in other words the stems of the creeper fully and abundantly crisscrossed the cemetery. The extended arms of the creeper started to bud and the buds would bloom into colourful flowers yielding fragrance for many miles. To enjoy this feast to the eyes, to imbibe the divine fragrance, my heart leapt and I waited for those days with uncontrollable impatience.

Suddenly the rhythm of nature turned upside down, the soothing gentle breeze ceased, and instead from the east came warm gusts of wind. The scorcher from the east squeezed in through the mountain passes and gaps unleashing a ruthless attack on the heights, the paradise on earth.

The flower beds of kurunjis wilted, leaving the remanets of a pyre reduced to ashes, and the grasslands degenerated into a colourless worn-out carpet. For the first time the heights sweated in a sultry atmosphere, and the residents carried fans, waving, them desperately to cool themselves. The tea gardens started to lose their vigour, the springs once considered as everlasting dried out fully, and the roar of the waterfall that echoed all over the year weakened and was reduced to a mere moan. For the first time, the pristine atmosphere of the heights got polluted by the fumes of forest fire.

The inhabitants of the heights were shocked and could not suppress their bewilderment; even the elderly adjudged these vagaries as previously unseen and unheard. Like a dancer with colours diluted and smudged on the face, the heights remained in depressed spirits. For souls with a poetic heart, the heights appeared like a beautiful woman turned grey and wrinkled overnight.

The scorching wind annoyed the heights with its jarring, ear-piercing whistle. Despite the adversities, we went ahead in full steam, brushing aside the threat of heat and forest fires. Putting out the embers of the burnt-down forests, we travelled fearlessly to different parts of the ranges to give relief to the unfortunate.

26

On a sultry night, I retired to the bedroom after prayers and dinner. Our incessant missionary activities kept the spirits of the vicar high and enabled him to recoup his health; it appeared to be the return of the vicar to his younger days.

Owing to the extreme humidity I was wearing light, cool clothes that night. While slowly immersing into slumber, the howling of the wild that proclaimed the presence of a huge pack of wild dogs at large in the heights knocked me up. The furniture in the room resonated to the high frequency of the blood-curdling song of the wild. I raised the flame of the lantern, then moved towards the glass window to observe the pitch dark exterior, and under the chorus of the wild even the framed window appeared resonating. I even feared that the sharp, shrill howling would pierce and shatter the glass window to pieces.

I looked through the window with eagerness and recollected my encounters with this diabolical experience twice in the past. The howling was on the ascent, and it appeared that it would never cease.

Suddenly the mass of swirling mist came to my attention; with horrifying thickness it hurtled towards the vicarage challenging the thick blanket of darkness. Finally, it came, slammed onto the glass window and enveloped the vicarage fully. Outside, the darkness turned white due to a heavy fog. The howling of the dogs reached incredibly dizzying heights. What prompted the wild to shake the heights with such intense howling which symbolizes death? The annoyance lasted many hours, shaking the heights to the core.

Gradually, the fog melted away and darkness regained dominance; the howling died down gradually and what remained was the sporadic moaning of the wild. It sounded like the pathetic, painful moaning of the dogs badly injured by fear.

While plunging to the depth of sound sleep Devassy knocked me up, and it was evident that something serious had happened.

In the living room, in the gleam of lantern, I found a man who was in a state of highest anxiety, and Esteppan was trying in vain to calm him down. The visitor, named Andraus, was the guard of the thriving dairy farm and he was forced to hasten to the vicarage at that inconvenient hour to communicate the strange incidents which had ocurred there a few hours ago. Devassy expressed his reluctance to disrupt the sound sleep of the elderly vicar, and that explains my presence in the living room at that odd hour.

I held his hand gently, looked at his face and gave a reassuring smile. Gradually he regained composure, and I made him sit on a chair; then drawing another chair I sat across from him, face to face. I maintained the gentle grip on his hand to ease the stress in his mind, but in spite of my sincere efforts and gestures of support, a fear still lingered in his mind.

Andraus presented a short sketch of the events which had unfolded in the dairy farm; owing to the lingering fear his account of the matter turned incoherent. The functioning of the diary farm had been extremely smooth till now and its reputation had been synonymous with efficiency and discipline. The diary farm had the reputation of being the ideal place to learn White Revolution, and it used to entertain thousands of researchers to the study of dairy industry. This phenomenal success boasted of a cattle population of more than a hundred varieties.

Every night, a team of three headed by Andraus guarded the farm. Till a few hours back everything had been going with clockwork precision. In the early hours of night everything was normal, the cattle grazed in comfort, swishing their tails to drive away the insects, but the scenario turned upside down when the ear-piercing howling surfaced from afar. The cattle grew uneasy with the intensity of the howling. When the mist enveloped the farm, they ran amok in fear. The well-organized farm turned into hell in an instant; running about in extreme fear, a few of them slammed onto the barbed-wire fence. Things started showing signs of improvement when the fog melted away and howling eased off.

I tried to cobble together a clear picture from the fragmented narrations. Esteppan prepared hot tea for Andraus and slowly he returned to normalcy. I decided to go to the dairy farm immediately with him, and took the lead by travelling on foot ahead of Andraus, holding a burning torch. In spite of it being a few hours before the break of dawn, the blanket of darkness which surrounded us looked impregnable, and I searched in vain for stars in the sky. We reached the farm in about half an hour and found the guards struggling hard to round-up the cattle on the loose. Some of them still wandered in the dark with severed ropes around their necks. With the aid of the light thrown by the burning torch, I assessed the damage immediately, and found at many places the fragments of shattered wooden planks. Many broken wooden posts stood as a grim reminder of the pandemonium which prevailed in the cattle shed. It appeared beyond doubt that the phenomenon which went past the heights was of a diabolical nature.

I returned to the vicarage when the white streaks of dawn appeared on the horizon. After prayers, I took breakfast merely for the sake of form and proceeded for mission activities. I remained virtually untouched by the string of events which had unfolded last night, and this acted as an indicator of the intensity of my faith in the Lord. After involving myself in the difficult activities of the mission, I came back to the vicarage in the evening. After evening prayers and dinner, I set off for the dairy farm with the blessings of the vicar. I went ahead brandishing the burning torch that diluted the darkness, and the air remained filled with the creaks of crickets; from the dense forest came the toot of a lone elephant. I proceeded with quick steps, and right at the entrance of the diary farm stood the trio awaiting my arrival impatiently. The anxiety on their faces conveyed their reluctance to spend another night at the farm in my absence. At my sight, they all heaved a long sigh of relief.

The gates of the farm closed behind me, and we all settled down in the guards' room. In the gleam of the lantern I observed every nook and corner of the room. There were bunk beds for the guards and another bed had been improvised for my comfort.

I sat by the lantern and opened the scriptures. In order to divert attention from the scary night, I concentrated on the Book of Jonah and read slowly. At every step, my heart throbbed with joy, as though tasting the drops of honey I enjoyed the love and affection of the Supreme Being that transcends the borders of the earth irrespective of caste, creed and religion. That night, like splitting hair, I studied the intricacies in the messages of the Almighty conveyed through Prophet Jonah.

Many hours passed, and at regular intervals the guards ensured that everything was under control through in the farm. The clock struck twelve and I continued meditating over the Book of Jonah. Each and every verse stood upright and proclaimed the boundless love of the Almighty. When the clock struck two I was meditating over the last chapter. Andraus expressed his optimism by ruling out the possibility of any strange events that night, and stretched himself on the bed.

A few minutes elapsed, from afar came the howling of the packs the sharpness of which sounded intensifying every second. With fear-stricken eyes, the trio sprang up and I stepped out of the room carrying the scriptures. The trio followed me with the lantern, and even the flame fluttered with the exasperation of the guards. The howling of the pack was on the ascent, and with an insatiable hunger to swallow everything, the phenomenon came drifting towards the cattle shed. The curls of the fog put in an appearance like a huge destructive power, and the the cows appeared uneasy; some of them tried to break away, swaying their heads violently. The cattle farm resembled a battle field, and the fear escalated to alarming levels.

I sang the verses of Psalm 91 and proclaimed the protection of the

Almighty; the howling of the packs reached the highest pitch, the surroundings came under the grip of a thick mist, but I kept on praying to the Lord. I fought against the strange phenomenon by shaping my faith in the form of a powerful weapon. Slowly the cattle settled down and uneasiness died down, but the howling of the wild, and the grip of the phenomenon lasted for half an hour. My prayers created a shield over the cattle shed and the cattle became calm. Finally, the phenomenon of mist started melting away, and the howling of the packs were on the descent. Eventually, the mayhem died down.

I reassured the trio, ruling out the possibility of any further upheavals in the cattle shed and left for the vicarage at the first streaks of dawn. I had immense confidence in the fortification of prayers raised around the dairy farm.

27

Palm Sunday arrived, and in the morning hundreds swarmed into the church with palm leaves. I assisted the vicar in the service that followed, and set off for mission work after the completion of sacraments. The Almighty filled my cells with energy in abundance, and on account of the blessings of the Lord my body transformed into an everlasting source of energy.

My destination was the aborigine settlement at the edges of the grassland. On the way, according to plan, a team of four joined me and we headed for the aborigine settlement, crossing the patch of grassland which had turned brown in the extreme heat. Slightly afar stood the tall trees of the forests.

We walked into the aborigine settlement, and the place looked deserted and under the blanket of silence. Suddenly there was a roar in the forests, the aborigines rushed out of the woods, dancing and swaying branches of trees, and after encircling us, they danced with abandon. It was a 'surprise' they had planned and executed well for us. With limited knowledge about Palm Sunday and limited resources, they celebrated Hosanna. Within a short time, we associated ourselves with the rhythm of the festivities. Salubrious atmosphere, well measured dance steps, the beats that exalt the spirits, and the swish of the branches in the air that carried the smell of greenery.

Involuntarily my thoughts travelled back to two thousand years ago, and the Mount of Olive in Jerusalem appeared within my ken. Thousands in exulted spirits, holding palm leaves swarmed to the road leading to Jerusalem. With radiance, they rolled out the garments, swayed palm leaves in rhythm, and in the gust of joy cried out 'Hosanna' to welcome the Son of God. I thought of myself as a humble servant of Christ, and waited impatiently to catch a glimpse of My Lord, and remained fully absorbed in the festivities. Gradually I drifted back to the present. The aborigines greeted us and did whatever they could to make us feel at home. We sat down and watched their dance.

A gentle breeze caressed us and we were engrossed in the festivities; the aborigines conveyed their overwhelming gratitude through the dance steps, and I thanked the Almighty who poured boundless joy into their hearts. Unthinkingly, my gaze flew up over the treetops and my heart fluttered in shock. Faraway the summit of the Dark Mountain blackened by the shadow of clouds stood in arrogance, and on that occasion, the peak seemed to posses more loftiness and blackness, representing the intensifying power of darkness.

In order to lessen the uneasiness, I turned my attention back to the festivities. The dance and the accompanying music went on for an hour and it turned out to be a perfect blend of Hosanna with traditional dance. I returned to the vicarage in the afternoon after completing the mission related activities scheduled on that day. While crossing the wide expanse of wilted grass, I threw a backward glance at the Dark Mountain and found the mountain still holding its head in arrogance. Its massive outline sowed the seed of apprehension in me, and the dense forests on the slopes remained partly hidden in the haze.

On my return, I sought refuge in the bedroom for recouping energy for the next seven hectic days. Evening prayers from Monday to Wednesday, then follows the Passover, the Good Friday and the culmination of Passion Week with the festivities of Easter.

I opened the scriptures, and an incident of great significance mentioned in the Gospel of Luke appeared before my eyes. The disciples of the Christ disputed to find out who was the greatest among them. Christ replies, 'The person who serves others like a servant deserves the title of the most superior.' My heart was deeply touched by the message, the last few months I had served others round the clock for Christ, enjoying every moment. I reached even the inaccessible remote aborigine localities, pulled out worms and blotted out puss from the body of the ailing souls riddled with wounds. I associated with the poor and the naked and served them as if serving the Almighty. Yet . . . is there still a blot in my mind? Do sin and trickery still germinate in the heart? Is my mind completely devoid of sin?

I glided through the streams of thoughts, twisting and turning, rising and plummeting, travelling through the complex maze of mind, and finally Esteppan through his untimely interference pulled me out of the journey. He conveyed the embarkation of the vicar on another severe fasting prayer, and handed over a written message from him which insisted for my presence in the meeting of the parish council to be held that night. It became evident that the vicar was struggling with a matter of utmost seriousness. With spiralling excitement, I waited for the commencement of the meeting.

The pall of darkness crept on to the heights before the advent of dusk. Because of the extreme humidity, contrary to usual, all the windows of the vicarage remained wide open. As if studded in the sky, the crescent and countless stars appeared. Most of the members of the parish council arrived after the fall of darkness, and the meeting commenced. The gleam of the lantern appeared inadequate in that atmosphere of utmost seriousness, and the vicar bore an exceedingly serious expression on his face. In addition to me, another member of the church was also present as a special invitee. The sole item on the agenda appeared terrifying and was a matter of great significance. The special invitee, Chackochan, was travelling through the large front yard of the church a couple of weeks back after midnight, and he was fearful and on the alert. On reaching the entrance of the cemetery, he threw a glance into the interiors and found something akin to a mist rising from the surface of the earth. According to his recollection it hovered around the spot close to the tomb of Tresa, and slowly assumed human form. He had the clear recollection of the cascading hair and the feet of the phenomenon slightly above the ground. Overwhelmed by intense fear, he screamed and fled, and while fleeing without proper sense of direction he faltered, fell and suffered injuries. I was shocked at the narrative of Chakochan, and all the members of the parish council present there appeared stupefied.

For a few moments silence remained predominant in the room, then, one of the committee members stated his view, which triggered a heated argument about how to bring about a permanent solution for this. The members of the committee informed the vicar of the invitation they had extended to the witch doctor of the Black Mountain and his willingness to come to destroy the spirit on Saturday next, the day before Easter. The vicar with my support launched a counter argument highlighting the incompatibility of such an action with our faith. Under pressure, the face of the vicar turned florid . . . his lips dried up, hands shivered, and I tried to keep his raging mind in check by holding on to his hand. The committee members stood their ground despite our intense persuasion, and conveyed the message powerfully that the invitation to the witch doctor was their personal decision and had nothing to do with the parish. They informed us to stay away from this matter since the witch doctor is capable of sacrificing the spirit without stepping into the church, and we ran out of solid grounds for opposing their scheme.

'Chacko, why did you go to the church in the middle of the night?' asked one member after a series of arguments.

'I went there just to enjoy the fresh air,' replied Chackochan with hesitation.

'Your house is almost two miles away from the church. Did you travel two miles at the dead of night just for the sake of enjoying fresh air?' asked another member and Chackochan remained speechless.

'He was unaware of the relocation of Susanna.' A member gifted with an excellent sense of humour launched a harpoon which shattered the defence of Chackochan.

The fear and anxiety melted away in an instant, and ripples of laughter echoed within the four walls of the room, and Chackochan turned pale noticeably even in the faint light in the room. The vicar sat serious and speechless, with a heart laden with sorrow.

Suddenly came from afar the faint howling of the pack; the huge waves of laughter ceased in an instant, and fear filled every inch of the room. The members of the parish council looked tense, and in that instant, it would have been difficult to judge whether their bodies were in full contact with the chairs on which they sat. The howling was on the ascent, the surroundings of the vicarage enveloped in the mist, and the phenomenon lasted for a quarter-hour, then eased off with the thinning out of the mist that we witnessed through the glass window. Gradually everything came back to normal.

'What causes this . . . so frequently?' asked one of the members of the committee.

'The power of darkness getting exalted,' said the vicar.

The members of the committee started to disperse, and the statement of the vicar triggered ripples of fear in me. From that moment, I started sensing the intensifying power of evil.

28

During the Passion Week, on Monday morning Esteppan woke me up and conveyed a message which almost shattered my heart. In an instant, I darted towards the cemetery, the iron gate of which was open. I spotted Devassy standing in the midst of tombs, he pointed towards the tomb of Tresa and my heart raced uncontrollably.

The creeper, which had carried the epithets of, 'everlasting' and 'invincible', appeared wilting; the arms which stretched to the corners of the cemetery coiled like leeches as if they came in contact with man. The buds on the tender leaves seemed destined for untimely death.

On account of intense heat, I sweated profusely. Ignoring the needling humidity, I scanned every corner of the cemetery closely. Like cancer, a yellowish tint kept spreading through the tender arms of the creeper. Slowly, I moved towards the tomb of Tresa, and noticed the green carpet of grass which was there in the cemetery a few weeks back had turned brown and colourless. In the hot wind, they swayed and sounded like fragments of metal scraping against one another.

The parts of the creeper which covered the tomb of Tresa still retained the green of the leaves. It appeared like an oasis in the vast expanse of a desert and the flowers shone like red rubies studded on velvet green. The vigour of the beautiful flowers calmed my heart. I sent Devassy back to the vicarage and sat on a stone next to the tomb, and at a distance appeared the summit of the towering peak which also appeared colourless instead of the luxuriance which had prevailed a few weeks ago. The slopes of the peak appeared stained with the blots caused by a series of forest fires.

I diverted my attention back to the creeper and caressed its leaves and stems, the aroma of divine flowers unwound my nerves which had been overstressed. I leaned towards the creeper, inserted both hands into the luxuriance, and enjoyed the feeling of the tightening grip of the stems and leaves on my hands. The divine flora triggered ripples of celestial bliss through my hands. Prompted by an urge to study the roots of the rare species, I pushed both hands into the depths of the creeper, tried to lift it, and found the attempt as difficult as lifting the mythological bow Saivachapam. I stood bent at the knees, amassed strength by arching the body forward, and again tried to lift the creeper with utmost difficulty. I clearly went through the feeling of the plant tightening its grip over me to grab and press my hands to the bosom of the tomb. Finally, with immense struggle, I raised the floral cover a bit and studied the roots.

Suddenly, something of immense interest struck my attention, and with a heart racing out of excitement I again raised the creeper slightly. For a moment, due to intense shock my heart seemed to be displaced by an inch, and I even doubted the credibility of my vision for the first time in life. The mother root of the creeper grew deep into the tomb piercing the marble surface on top, and it became evident that the origin of the mother root was in the heart of Tresa. With a start I fell back, and the creeper rested back onto the tomb with a slight moan. I returned to the vicarage with a lightened heart to brace myself up for the evening service.

In the church, that night the candle flames struggled to keep the darkness at bay. Despite the sultry uncomfortable air, the congregation associated themselves with the persecutions suffered by the Almighty. As a parish, we mustered ourselves for the commemoration of the crucifixion of Christ. On the next morning I visited Tresa's tomb accompanied by Devassy, the outcome of which turned out to be extremely disappointing. The yellowish colour had consumed more than half of the arms of the creeper, and I feared the wilting process would affect even the roots of the flora. Devassy attributed the sudden change to the extremely dry conditions of the heights. I instructed him to water the creeper at regular intervals giving special care to the roots piercing the soil.

The next day the weather worsened, pushing the mercury to new heights; the scorching wind from the east grew intense, and for the first time in history, the heights appeared uninhabitable. I set off towards the cemetery in the morning and found a few more heart-breaking incidents in store for me. Despite careful nursing, the condition of the creeper appeared worsened with the weariness spreading to the heart of the flora that covered Tresa's tomb. The blooms on the tomb appeared colourless, and the signs of weariness were obvious.

In spite of adverse weather, the congregation responded to the activities of Passion Week overwhelmingly, and the enthusiastic response bolstered my confidence and kept expectations alive.

After midnight, the nagging needles of humidity disrupted my sleep. In spite of leaving the windows open, my body remained fully drenched in sweat. The circumference of the moon appearing through the window heralded the outset of Passover. I raised the flame of the lantern and unfolded the scriptures. My mind was in extreme turbulence on account of the creeper which was on the decline, and I felt the powers of darkness growing sky high.

To mitigate the effects of turbulence in my heart, I started journeying through the scriptures, and the verses turned the clock back to the first century of Christian era. The city of Jerusalem was drenched in the full moon and appeared in my ken; I saw the silhouette of a group of people in an ill-illuminated chamber. After washing the feet of the disciples, Christ proceeded to the Garden of Gethsemane with them. The Mount of Olive assumed sharpness in my vision and I clearly saw the protruding branches of olive trees in the backdrop of the full moon. Christ went a little further away from the disciples, and his heart-shattering, pain-stricken utterances of prayers lashed my ears like thunder. Due to intense grief the drops of sweat turned blood. Drawing strength from prayer, he had braced up for the most difficult mission of death on the cross. Then he had got arrested by the Roman soldiers and the disciples had scattered in fear like a flock without a shepherd.

I felt an uneasy heaviness in my chest, and found once again the tower of faith unstable. Like the faith of the disciples who had conversed with Christ for nearly three years and still fled, my faith also appeared totally inept. At crucial junctures, the disciples failed in the test of faith. Feeling the deficiencies in my faith, I knelt and prayed. Gradually my mind returned to normalcy, or in other words, heaven strengthened my heart.

The morning of Passover arrived, and with a sinking heart and weary mind I reached the cemetery immediately after the first streaks of dawn on the horizon. The entire creeper appeared weary and without vigour. The evil yellow had already made inroads into the very heart of the creeper. The leaves started coiling on account of wilting, and the flowers looked unattractive and colourless.

I instructed Devassy to water the creeper more often, but he totally disregarded my suggestion on the saying that the creeper was getting disintegrated on account of excessive watering. He strongly recommended leaving the plant undisturbed for a natural death.

With a shattered heart and bowed head I returned from the cemetery. On account of the disorientation triggered by the aching heart, I was forced to support myself on the headstones for balance. That day turned out extremely scorching. I mitigated my pains in the heart through prayers, and braced myself for the service of Passover which is of great significance.

In the evening, the flames of the candles sprouted in the altar, and challenging the extreme humidity many swarmed into the church for the service of Passover. The vicar, totally overcoming the challenges of his advanced age, spearheaded the service with amazing perfection.

His voice did not quiver, nor did his hands shiver, and the stoop appeared fully vanished. His voice echoed on the walls of the church like the roar of a lion, and in a commanding voice he called upon the congregation to cast away arrogance and selfishness, then to wash the feet of the brethren like Christ. That evening, the unwavering faith of the vicar acted as the perfect crutches for me to limp forward through the terrain of spiritual challenges.

After the service I returned to the vicarage, changed into fresh clothes, and set off for a stroll to find relief from the annoying humidity that prevailed in the full moon of Passover. The sky appeared extremely luminous in the radiance of moonlight. Against the backdrop of the illuminated sky, the silhouette of the church, its belfry, and the towering roof emerged. I walked through the parched extensive front yard of the church, and sat on the wall bordering the tea gardens. The ranges appeared like a silver wall; in the moonlight the colourless carpet of the tea garden looked as though striving to regain the lost elegance of the place and I sat watching the cloud flakes drifting through the sky.

29

Alone, fully drenched in moonlight I embarked on meditation. Two thousand years back, on a night of immensely radiant moonlight, the city of Jerusalem witnessed many a landmark historical event. Right in front of my eyes emerged the Garden of Gethsemane, the branches of the olives against the backdrop of the full moon appeared like the strokes of a paint brush. I clearly saw the flash and undoubtedly heard the hiss of a sword. The scream of agony of the Roman soldier whose ear got severed pierced my eardrums. My heart leapt at the sigh of relief let out by the man whose severed ear got moulded back by the miracle-working hands of Christ. I vividly made out the denials of Peter and clearly heard the crowing of the rooster. The restrained sobs of Peter touched my heart. I shuddered at the hiss and swish of the whips, and my heart literally wept at the anguished cries of my Lord.

With an earth-shattering scream, I came back to the present. As if afflicted by the unbearable emotional pain, the moon concealed its face behind the flakes of clouds, and the ranges made themselves invisible under the fading moonlight. My heart wept. With a mind-throbbing in pain, I returned to the vicarage.

The dawn of Good Friday. In the morning, the church got inundated by hundreds of believers. From the altar, it looked like a large thick human canopy, through which even a grain of sand could not percolate down. In the extremely sultry air, the church turned itself into an oven. On that day, I clearly comprehended the intensity of the vicar's faith. He led the most significant service which spanned many hours, outlasting the challenges of advanced age, and his chanting appeared as rising from the depths of the heart.

The service advanced to the Stations of Cross which unfolded the series of significant events in the history of the world. After issuing the verdict to crucify Jesus Christ, Pontius Pilate the governor washed his hands; the soldiers of the governor put a scarlet robe on him, and hammered the crown of thorns onto his head. I remained completely immersed in the service, and clearly heard the swishing of Roman whips.

Christ, laden with the heavy cross, then moves towards the 'Place of Skull' suffering innumerable falls and persecutions on the way. I clearly heard the roar of the crowd, and staggered at the thud of the heavy cross on the firm ground.

My heart never throbbed so vehemently, despite having attended Good Friday services since childhood. Right in my vision, a strange invisible force turned the clock two millennia back. The narrow paths of Jerusalem appeared in my sight, slightly afar; out of the city gates stood Golgotha, the laughter of the Romans, and the sharp metallic clang of nails pierced my ears. I shivered at the thud of hammer and shuddered at the anguished cries of my dearest Lord; drops of blood flew in the air and splattered onto my face, scalding my eyes and blurring my vision. I almost collapsed onto the floor under intense agony; thousands of believers imbibed the essence of death on the cross, many eyes became tearful, many voices quivered in intense grief, and finally, the church service which touched the heart of multitudes came to a conclusion.

The congregation dispersed after partaking in the humble meals arranged by the parish council. After returning to the vicarage, changing my clothes in a flash, I hurtled towards the cemetery. Overhead, the sun burned with a vengeance, and in the strong waves of the scorching wind mirages emerged, shocking me to the core. I turned apprehensive about the possibility of annihilation of this beautiful piece of land by the merciless deeds of nature. In the cemetery, much darker events were awaiting me; the death of the creeper appeared almost complete, and like an octopus with thousands of tentacles appeared the remains of the wilted creeper on the tomb of Tresa. With a shattered heart I knelt down near the tomb. The wilted flowers and the blades of grass murmured jarringly in the sultry wind.

There appeared a rising framework slightly away from the cemetery; in the refraction of the mirage it looked like patches of smudged ink, and it took much straining of my eyes to discern the framework as a structure with thatched roof being made. My sorrows intensified at the realization that the thatched structure symbolized the end of the phenomenon that was Tresa. The sudden rush of grief squeezed my heart and the insatiable desire to view that most beautiful face intensified in me, my mind throbbed to feel the gentle, divine touch again. I resolved to save her soul from the evil fire of the witchdoctor at any cost.

I darted out of the cemetery like a wild horse. Under my feet, dry blades of grass hissed like snakes. In a wink, I crossed the long front yard of the church and plunged into the wide expanse of the tea gardens. The half-wilted tea plants left scratches on my body hissing, and I dashed through the narrow intricate paths.

I snaked and squeezed through the challenges raised by the boulders. At the edge of the forest, instead of the impregnable green curtain, I encountered the dry walls of nature which was in absolute ruins, and the undergrowth remained fully wilted. I ran through the bed of the forest, mercilessly trampling on them; the dried leaves screeched under my feet . . . the snapping of twigs sounded likes the breaking of bones. The sharp dry branches and stems raised formidable challenges to my safety, but like a skilled Kalari fighter, I evaded their sharp tips. The scorching day had blotted out the springs and streams from the bed of the forest. Traversing through this vast pyre of nature, I reached the banks of the stream.

The stream which used to flow in boundless torrents appeared like a worn-out shadow, and I ran upstream parallel to the brook. Even while dashing through the forest, I desperately searched for the divinely face. The leaves on the trees seemed to form a shield, and tried to save me from the wrath of the sun.

Till recently, the interiors of the forest thrived with fauna and flora, but what existed now were the mere fossils of life. I came closer to the once thriving waterfall and shuddered at the vision I saw. The movement of my legs came to a grinding halt, right before me appeared a wall of rock chiselled by the torrent over millennia, and on the wall of rock like a very thin thread appeared the remains of the waterfall. The energetic, roaring cascade of water was no longer in existence, and nature, which had symbolized elegance, appeared like a whore who is scantily clad. That was the end of my dreams. My head dropped, shoulders sagged, legs started to give way, and losing my balance I landed into the almost dry stream with a thud. In my disoriented senses and fading memory, I found the sparse canopy of the trees above spinning like a top.

Finally I regained consciousness, then slowly got up and tried to quench my thirst by cupping water from the stream. For a few moments, I searched unsuccessfully for Tresa then headed back to the vicarage with a shattered heart. The sunlight appeared appreciably weakening in the forest and signalled the untimely arrival of darkness. I was well aware of the remaining few hours before dusk, and considered the fading of sunlight as something unearthly. The birds tried to return to their nests and the pack of monkeys expressed their uneasiness through nagging screeches. It was clear that the wildlife was not at ease at the untimely encroachment of darkness. I hastened my steps with an intention to leave the forest before the disappearance of the last speck of light.

At every step the sunbeams appeared waning, affecting the visibility considerably. On certain occasions, I travelled fumbling through the fading light. I was apprehensive of losing my way and ending up in the remotest part of the forest. Finally, much to my relief appeared the boulders indicating the right direction. In a leap, I reached the top of the boulders and from there cast a wide glance towards the horizon. In the west, the sun was getting obscured under a strange phenomenon like mist.

Afar the ranges appeared as illegible outlines; like the sketch of a painter stood the belfry and the tower of the church, and the wilted carpet of tea gardens appeared as depressing as a cremation ground.

Under the strange phenomenon, the sun was almost obscured, and appeared fragile and frail. My thoughts travelled upstream through the channels of time. I had a clear vision of the darkness which had come over Judea two millennia back, and stood shocked at the vision of the crosses at Golgotha against the grim backdrop of the sky. The earth shook and the rocks shattered. I vividly felt the rumbling of the earth under my feet, and even feared the collapse of the ranges in the tremor. A powerful wind which appeared from nowhere kicked streams of dust up to the sky; the half wilted canopy of tea gardens swayed raising the scrapping sound of metal blades. As if I had caught a glimpse of a monster I hurtled towards the vicarage, screaming.

30

Pushing the door open violently, I rushed into the vicarage. The oddity of my entry made Esteppan and Devassy very uneasy. Without any words, I withdrew myself into the bedroom. It seemed that the heights were under the vice-like grip of fear.

I refused to have dinner due to the turbulence in my mind. After raising the flame of the lantern, I unfolded the scriptures. The juggernaut of time turned two millennia back into the past. The body of Christ was buried temporarily in the tomb owned by Joseph of Arimathea, and a huge rock bearing the unbreakable seal of the Caesar stood at the mouth of the tomb. To entomb the legend of Jesus forever guards were deployed at the entrance of the cave.

Each and every verse from the scriptures appeared in the form of images, and the images of fear-stricken disciples emerged in my mind vividly. With sagging shoulders, they sat fearing even a faintest gleam of light. My heart struggled in grief, and I tried to push the feeling of pessimism back with the sword of faith, but my frustrations intensified with the passage of time.

The long service of Good Friday and the journey in haste to the waterfall in very hot conditions had taken its toll on me. I slowly drifted into the deepest sleep in weariness.

Next day, I woke up late and found the room well illuminated by bright sunbeams. With a start I got up and hastened to the cemetery. I shivered violently at the sight I encountered on the tomb of Tresa.

The creeper was no longer alive, and I cried at the top of my voice at the death of the divine plant.

The completed structure with the thatched roof stood at a distance in arrogance, symbolizing the possibility of early commencement of rituals to annihilate the spirit of Tresa once for all. Prompted by the desire to protect her from the rituals, I ran out of the cemetery and reached the edge of the forest in a flash.

After traversing the forest bed like lightning, I darted to the grassland which appeared brown at the height of the summer. The towering peak afar bore the expression of an emperor stripped of his glory. Stamping on the sharp blades of grass, I made my way towards the peak and even injured my feet. The radiance of the sun intensified and baked me in acute heat; in the hot humid wind, the grassland swayed, blurting out evil mantras. Almost drained of energy on reaching the base of the peak, I landed on my face on the ground due to a terrible fall. After gaining a slight reprieve, I lapped up like a dog the puddle of unclean water that I sighted in the vicinity.

After a short rest, my heart rate eased; then I threw an upward glance towards the summit and found the dry steep slope . I nursed the hope of finding the angelic face of Tresa somewhere in the summit and this hope acted as a strong motivator. Amassing the last quantum of energy I negotiated the steep slopes. Unlike usual, the mist was totally absent; instead, I suffered under the attack of the sun which rained down sharp arrows on me. My skin suffered sunburn, and I struggled hard to scale the peak amidst extremely adverse circumstances.

During the ascent, I looked upwards and had a clear view of the summit which appeared like the forehead of an elephant. I kept on climbing fast and soon found myself only a stone's throw away from the summit—then stooping the head, bending the shoulders, I hurtled towards the zenith. The tendons on the legs, stretching like a string, inflicted excruciating pain. Finally, with a powerful jerk and shattering the chains of gravity, I gained the top of the peak. My lungs appeared empty under the severe stress. My legs gave way, and I landed on the parched surface losing the balance—then, slowly, I glided down into the world of reveries.

In the faint gleam appeared the interior of a room with doors and windows strongly barred. Slowly, the images of a few men who wore a depressing expression emerged. Even in the insufficient light, I was able to assimilate the intensity of the pain and humiliation on their faces. A few of them sat like people devoid of hope and rested their heads on the palm. Since heavily laden with the bitterness of failure, they even started at the faintest waves of sound. The atmosphere appeared thick with grief and utter disappointment.

I regained consciousness and opened my eyes. The sun was slanting westwards. I got up in haste. What I had witnessed a few moments back appeared more than a dream. My mind associated the men with the crestfallen disciples of Christ and their melancholy expression with their shattered confidence.

I stepped onto the highest point in the summit; in the strong wind came the surprising needles of chill and my clothes fluttered. I indulged in a futile and desperate search for Tresa. Once again I desperately yearned for the sight of the palms embossed with nail marks. When the efforts turned futile, I felt even heaven had turned its face away from me. The Dark Mountain with its oily darkness was clearly visible from the zenith, and that image conveyed the disturbing message of the impending dominance of evil over the divine.

A dark speck appeared in the western horizon and it kept on enlarging every moment. I realized that the dark speck in the horizon was a vast army of clouds marching onto the heights. The rituals would have started near the cemetery, and within hours the spirit of Tresa would be consumed in fire for ever. The very thought of this impending disaster propelled me through the steep declivity. Whenever threatened by the possibility of losing balance, I crawled down with the flexibility of reptiles and agility of monkeys. After the extremely dangerous descent, I ran like a cheetah through the grassland. It appeared that the wind carried moisture in stark contrast to the heat that was there a few hours back.

The army of clouds coming from the west moved swiftly through the air, and their presence lightened the intensity of the sun. The conquest of the clouds reached above the grassland. On account of the thickness of the clouds, I remained apprehensive of the possibility of the collapse of the dark canopy onto the grassland. The cold wind laden with abundant moisture started lashing, and the swaying knee-high grass blades appeared like millions of provoked serpents.

I darted against the wind that gained momentum steadily. The tall trees in the forests edging the grass land swayed violently and I dashed into the midst of trees at an alarming speed. In the dimness of the forest bed, I ran forward with fumbling steps. The intensifying wind blew thousands of dry leaves from the forest bed, the leaves of the tall trees shuddered and some of the heavy branches snapped in the wind and came crashing down. I emerged from the dimness of the forest, and I hurtled through the sea of parched tea gardens, which moved like waves in the wind.

Against the backdrop of the overcast sky appeared the towering belfry of the church. My insane dash culminated on the front yard of the church and from there I turned back and cast a fearful glance at the scene. Legions of huge clouds were scraping into the ranges. Hysterically the trees in the forest swayed and the tea gardens seemed like the surface of a raging dark sea.

Sensing the impending danger, I ran into the church and climbed the maze of twisting and turning stairs to the part of roof next to the belfry. In the violent wind, the dangling bell rope swung uncontrollably; in the gust of air the metallic tongue of the bell scraped against the metal cast emitting faint waves of frequent chimes. I stormed on to the roof that commanded an excellent view of the cemetery, and the sight of the thatched structure, the ritual fire and the swaying flames shook me to the core. The lashing wind pushed me away and to protect myself from being blown away, I held firmly on to the banister.

The humongous army of rainclouds conquered the four corners of the sky with ease, streaks of lightning crisscrossed like venomous snakes, and the earth shook under the impact of a powerful thunder. In an instant, the drizzle turned to shower, and shower turned to rain, and the rain turned into a destructive cloudburst. Hailstones battered onto roofs and scattered. Within a short time, the church complex became encircled with pure white crystals of ice.

The powerful winds turned into a storm and the storm dismantled the thatched structure throwing fragments all over; the ritual flames spiralled up alarmingly, and in the howling of the wind, the horizons stood fearfully. Then came the series of lightning and thunder of greatest intensity. The tall deep-rooted trees in the forests swayed like frail bushes, and a turbulence of this magnitude appeared unparalleled in the history of the heights. Suddenly the deadly arm of a lightning flew down from the sky, and close on its heels came the crash of a powerful thunder that sounded like an explosion. A pillar of fire appeared on the ground where the thatched structure stood a few moments back, and that moment I realized the demise of the ritual fire by a fatal lightning.

The long series of thunder and lightning continued, raindrops as big as globes slammed onto the ground as if determined to shatter the earth. Then emerged from the dizzying heights of the sky another arm of lightning and triggered a powerful explosion in the bell tower. Shocked to the hilt, I looked upwards and found fragments of tiles flying in the air. Suddenly a large projectile appeared out of nothing flying towards me. I suffered a terrible slap on my face, and I felt like gliding in the air under the impact of the blow.

31

A kaleidoscope of smudges of colours emerged before me; slowly it took the appearance of blotted images; gradually the images sharpened and turned into the objects of enticement. The vast canopy of the sky remained azure without a stain of cloud. Slowly crept into my ken, the shattered belfry of the church, and I came back to my senses.

Slowly I raised my head and sat for a while without realizing the significance of the day, 'the Easter'. Every part of my body wriggled under acute pain. Gradually my reason came back to me.

The heightened senses thrust a harpoon into my heart. I made an attempt to rise, but failed, lost ground and collapsed onto the floor. With immense effort I raised myself supporting on the banister, then holding onto the railings tried to descend the flight of stairs. At every step, my body wriggled in acute pain and every movement triggered unbearable agony akin to hammering nails into my head. Swaying, shivering and falling I managed to snake down the stairs. My heart throbbed with excruciating pain worrying about the fate of Tresa. Sobbing uncontrollably I limped towards the cemetery.

I struggled to endure the intensifying sorrow. With the fuming desire to weep embracing the lifeless parts of the creeper, I kept on moving forward heedless of the piercing pain triggered by every step. Before my eyes appeared the entrance to the cemetery severely damaged by the storm last night. In order to receive and consume the bitter chalice of sorrow I moved into the cemetery on the morning of the Easter.

At the sight of something incredible, my heart galloped; in an instant, my spirits spiralled from the abyss of hopelessness to the dizzying heights of bliss. I even doubted my senses for a while. I rubbed my eyes to ensure the sight was not a mere illusion.

In a flash the pain and uneasiness eased off; limping and jumping, I plodded through the cemetery. The elegance of the creeper which had reconquered every inch of the cemetery provided a perfect feast for my eyes. Every nook and corner of the cemetery shone in the abundance of flowers. The flower bed had been expanded to the length and breadth of the cemetery, and the creeper looked no longer inanimate.

I knelt near the tomb of Tresa. The thriving leaves and flowers turned the cemetery into a beautiful carpet studded with emerald and diamonds. The branches coiled onto my body, the flowers stretched forward and planted thousands of kisses coated with immeasurable fragrance.

In the light breeze, basking in the warmth of the morning sun, my cells reformed into the reservoir of energy which would equip me to travel along the path of the divine, untiringly, throughout my life. I turned my attention back to the landscape. The towering peak beamed in lush greenery, and the heavy rains restored the tint of silver on the ranges. The thick forest reappeared as the dense fortress of greenery.

I raised my eyes to heaven and thanked the Almighty from the depths of my heart. Like the disciples of Christ overjoyed by the resurrection, I experienced inexplicable bliss. Henceforth no more apprehensions . . . no more fear . . . no more hesitations . . . but a consistent, unwavering journey along the path of the divine.

I turned my gaze on the creeper, the arms and leaves of which resembled the body and the bright red flowers symbolized the wounds of Christ. The thick green leaves and stems firmly coiled around me. I underwent the vivid sensation of the hands imprinted with nail marks holding me close and caressing me with overflowing affection. This experience of the divine would enable me to traverse thousands of miles in the mission of serving my Lord.

I, Yousuf Yesudas, student of theology and aspirant to priesthood, opened my heart with immense joy and prayed to the Almighty for the boon of being able to identify Christ in the poor, naked and distressed. I clearly felt the waves of prayers scaling incredible heights and knocking on the gates of heaven. Under its impact the sky and the earth stood in reverence.

GLOSSARY OF A FEW MALAYALAM AND SPECIALIZED ENGLISH WORDS USED IN THIS WORK

Blouse & Kaili
The women's dress of peasants in Kerala.

Gandeevam
A mythical bow mentioned in the epic *Mahabharata* which is capable of increasing a single arrow to thousands on release.

Heights (The Heights)
An imaginary place that has a striking resemblance to Munnar, a hill station located in the Western Ghats in Kerala at an altitude ranging from 1450 metres to 2700 metres above sea level.

Kalari
The ancient martial art of Kerala.

Kavacham & Kundalum
The inherited and inherent Armour and Earring of the great legendary warrior Karna that provided him invincibility as described in the epic *Mahabharata*.

Kerala
One of the states in India located at the southernmost tip of the Indian peninsula and renowned for its natural beauty that has earned the state the sobriquet 'God's own Country'

Kuttanadu
Part of Kerala that is below sea level, crisscrossed with innumerable canals, tributaries and rivers.

Lord Varuna
The Hindu god of rain and water.

Malayalam
The official language of the State of Kerala, spoken by 35 million people in India.

Mundu & Jubba
The traditional lily-white men's dress of Kerala.

Muziris
An ancient port in Kerala which Roman ships used to frequent for spices, ivory and wood. Doubting Thomas, a disciple of Christ, is believed to have disembarked here for proclaiming the gospel through the length and breadth of Kerala.

Neelakurunji (*Strobilanthes kunthiana*)
A rare species of plant that grows abundantly in the vicinity of Munnar and blooms only once in 12 years.

North East Monsoon
The retreating monsoon in the Indian subcontinent active from October to November. The rains are usually accompanied by deadly lightings and thunder.

Othiram and Poozhi Kadakam
Techniques in the Kalaripayattu, the ancient martial art of Kerala.

Saivachapam
Mythical bow at the swayamvaram of Sita mentioned in the epic *Ramayana*.

South West Monsoon
The monsoon active from June to September. This period is marked by heavy to very heavy rainfall without lightning and thunder.

Western Ghats
The mountain range running through the western coast of India. This range starts from Gujarat and ends in Kanya Kumari, the southernmost tip of India.

ACKNOWLEDGMENTS

I express my boundless gratitude to my dearest father, KM George, and my dearest mother, Saramma George, who embellished my imagination from a tender age with Indian Epics and Bible stories respectively.

I thank my Brother, Cecil George Mathew, who helped me to take my first steps in the world of imaginations.

I express my appreciation for my wife, Ivy, who took the trouble of compiling, preserving and safeguarding the manuscripts over a decade like a cache of treasures, nullifying the negatives of my disorderly writing style.

My special thanks to Dudley Cowan of Springfield Lakes Toastmasters Club, Devassia Thottunkkal of River Rock Real Estate—Boronia Heights, John Thomas (Reji) and the late Lawrence Bain who all selflessly travelled many extra miles in turning this book into a reality.

I thank the members of the Springfield Lakes Toastmasters Club for finetuning my communication skills and inculcating confidence to proceed with the book.

I thank my forefathers Mahakavi KV Simon, Mahakavi Edayaranmula KM Varghese and Prof KM Daniel for their boundless blessings.

I bow my head before the memories of the Late Mrs Rachel Thomas, the former editor of *Manorajyam Weekly* who despite being on her death-bed persuaded me not to give up writing.

I kneel before the Almighty for the stream of imagination and apt words that constitute the fabric of this work.

ABOUT THE AUTHOR

Cyril George Joseph was born in India and lived in Abu Dhabi for seventeen years before migrating to Australia in 2008. He is married with three children, and currently lives at Springfield. *The Mysteries of the Heights* is his debut English novel.